Hunter eased up slowly, taking deep breaths to steady his voice. He had been shot at countless times when he served in the Royal Navy, but one never grew used to such an experience. Adrenaline tempered his nerves, and after a second breath he looked down at the terrified children.

"Both ok?"

He was rewarded by a pair of nodding, grimy faces drawn with lines of hunger and fear. From the hatch, William's panic-white face peered over the edge and looked skyward. Behind him, O'Fallon had already drawn a pistol and true to his nature, looked for a chance to soothe his anger. Moira however, was not within sight.

"Good, now a brief introduction. I'm Captain Anthony Hunter of the *Brass Griffin* and this is my crew. We're here to help."

Immediately, the children screamed again.

Tales of the Brass Griffin: A Children's Tale

C. B. Ash

2

A Children's Tale

Other fine books by C. B. Ash:

Kinloch Novels:

Kinloch

Tales of the Brass Griffin Novels:

Red Lightning
Children's Tale
Dead Air
Bloody Business
Dead Men's Tales
The Seventh Knife*

*Currently viewable on http://brassgriffin.com

TALES OF THE BRASS GRIFFIN: A CHILDREN'S TALE

Copyright © 2013 by Christopher B Ash

ISBN: 978-0-578-03615-1

First Edition: August 2009
Second Edition: Sept 2013

Cover by: Jeroen ten berge (http://jeroentenberge.com/)

For Zoe and Ryan,
I hope you always find an adventure around every corner.

Chapter 1

This high in the mountains the sky was almost featureless. Clouds spread across the stretch of sky like a gray, padded gauze that filtered the sunlight to a muted, smoky dawn. A gust of wind touched with the damp cold of rain and snow stirred the rigging and trim sails around the main gas bag. On the deck, the crew busied themselves with their daily tasks, only today they kept a watchful eye on the stretch of snow capped mountains that loomed nearby and below the ship itself.

Captain Hunter, dressed in his usual dark trousers, boots, shirt and long coat leaned on the starboard railing. Quietly he scanned the mountainside below, almost oblivious to his surroundings. Finally, struck by some odd thought, he withdrew a folded piece of paper from his coat breast pocket. He unfolded the worn correspondence, then read the message again.

"*My dear Captain Anthony Hunter,*

My associates speak highly after you and word of the reputation of you and your crew speaks likewise of your merit. I seek your employment on a matter of some import. Perhaps you are familiar with her, but the ship Marie Celeste *has been logged overdue for arrival at Port Camden. This is of great concern to me as I had booked passage for my own niece and nephew to travel to meet their long lost parents. As I have been their caretaker for some time now, naturally I am concerned as to their outcome.*

Enclosed is a map that detailed the last route taken by the Marie Celeste and a Bill of Order detailing the amount I have advanced. This first amount is up front for you and your crew's efforts. Any news will garner a similar amount upon your return.

Yours with gratitude,

Ian Von Patterson"

The captain brushed a few snowflakes that fell on the paper then folded it thoughtfully. Last calculations put them along the same route as the *Marie Celeste*, seven days out from London. He sighed and surveyed the rocky ground covered in a fresh blanket of snow. The wind stirred again and the *Brass Griffin* creaked in reply, a protest against the weather while the ship gently banked to port.

From the quarterdeck came a shout from the navigator, Billy Baker. Baker was a thin man with deep gray eyes and nimble way with his hands. Rumor had it that Billy's mother was a sea witch and he inherited some of the Gift from her. Billy himself only would say he had a knack for finding things. "Ship ahead!"

Captain Hunter stood up and returned the letter to his breast pocket. He called back, "How's she fare Mr Baker?"

"The bird's aground Cap'n, a good 10 twain down on that snow and tree covered slope. Not sure she'll fly again without some work."

"Any sign of castaways?"

"None Cap'n, but tha' don't mean there's not any."
Hunter nodded to himself, the lad was right about that one. "Thank you,

Mr Baker."

A rough voice preceded Hunter's first mate while he joined the captain at the rail. "Our employer won't like this. He was clear about finding the children alive."

"We don't know the *Marie Celeste* went down and took all hands and passengers with her, Krumer." Hunter scrutinized the mountainside until his eyes caught sight of the downed airship. He let out a small whistle of amazement at the view of the mangled wreck. The first mate shook his head slowly at the sight. "Her gas bag's in at least four parts, and it looks like she hit bow-first when she came in. She might have weathered it, but that large rock outcrop sheared her like a knife. It'd have been rough to ride her down."
"What would your Orcish spirits say about those odds?"

A grin spread across Krumar's flat orcish face, he folded his heavily muscled arms over his chest, straining his worn white shirt. "They'd remind me they don't believe in the odds. Me? I'd say even odds here. If the ones in the stern didn't get bounced around too much when she hit and if she just didn't collapse on herself when she ran aground."

The pilot brought the ship around again, closer this time, to offer a better look at the wrecked airship below. On this pass, the crew's usual work on the rigging and other matters slowed while all looked over the side towards the scene. No one spoke more than a whisper or two out of respect for the deceased spirits of passengers and what the crew believed was the deceased spirit of a wrecked airship. Even the regular protests of the *Griffin* herself sounded mournful and quiet while they passed.

It was Hunter who broke the spell of silence. "That's a bloody large set of 'ifs', Mr. Whitehorse."

"Aye Cap'n. I'll take them too, if it means we've live survivors to return instead of dead remains."

"Some hope is better than none, eh? Well, I'll take that." Hunter turned towards the knot of crew that had gathered at the port rail. "Mr. O'Fallon?"

The broad shouldered, tattooed man with a long red pony tail near the back of the group looked over. "Aye Cap'n?"

"Bring out the longskiff, I'll be taking three down ashore with me to search the wreck."

"Aye Cap'n."

The red haired quartermaster looked at the crew. "Ye both there and ye by the rail. Ye'll be doin' in a pinch. Ya be hearin' the captain, he be wantin' his longskiff. Look alive!"

Quickly the three men, escorted by O'Fallon, raced to the winch towards the bow where the longskiff was folded and stowed. Once the ropes were released, the four men slowly drew the catamaran shaped craft up over the railing and unfolded the second smaller boat hull that provided some storage and ballast to the first. The cold wind rippled the longskiff's kite sails while a small flock of brightly colored firehawks swooped and played among the top rigging of the *Griffin* herself. Firehawks, modest sized birds that were a stout foot from toe to shoulder with fiery orange and red feathers, often enjoyed the heated updrafts of air from an airship's steam engines.

Hunter walked to the port rail next to the few crew that

remained there. Slowly he shook his head in sad dismay at the tangled knots of rope, wood and bodies that littered the white, clean snow.

"A lot of 'ifs', Krumer, a lot of them."

Chapter 2

Clouds of steam erupted around the longskiff when it slid to a stop on the packed snow. The whine of turbines echoed with a haunting cry among the wreckage of gas bag, pieces of wood, brass, rigging and spots of blood. When the longskiff came to a rest, O'Fallon jumped out, pulled the bowline and lashed the craft to a nearby tree. He tugged at his dark wool coat around him and turned just as the wind stirred the snow in small clouds around his boots. Captain Hunter followed the quartermaster a moment later, his eyes swept over the upthrust pieces of wood and bent brass fittings.

"Quite the mess here," Hunter commented.
O'Fallon tugged at the mooring line and, convinced it secure, took in his own view of the wreckage with a sigh. "She took quite the beating, nothing more'n grapeshot, but a large sight 'o it." He knelt and pulled a dented brass object from where it lay half-buried. Shaking the snow loose, he turned the sextant over in his hands before he handed it to Hunter. The captain turned it over himself while Moira and William vented the steam which powered down the air screws and reduced the tension in the longskiff's gas bag.

"Lets spread out. O'Fallon, you and William take starboard. Moira, you're with me here at the bow."

O'Fallon nodded then gave the younger William Falke a reassuring grin. "Let's see who be layin' about."

William sighed and managed a smile although his eyes still swept the ruined ship with a look of dismay. The young man rubbed his gloved hands together to beat off the cold, then pulled his gray woolen coat tighter around him before he followed O'Fallon's boot tracks.

When the pair had left, Moira sighed. Dressed in a leather long coat, warm shirt, trousers and her usual well worn boots, she was suited to the weather but not the scene before her. She shook her head slowly and put her hands on her hips. "The bow's a mess Cap'n. Nothin' be livin' through that."

"Likely as so, but we still need to check. An then there is funeral detail for the crew and what passengers they had. Might have to dig for a few that would've been buried by the impact of the crash. They all deserve at least that."

Moira cast a somber look at the scattered remains of the former merchant ship then recovered her canvas shoulder bag of small tools from the longskiff. Light snow fell softly on the broken, bloodstained wood and covered the few ruined bodies of victims that had been thrown clear during the crash. "Aye Cap'n. Ah'll look for personal items ta try and return ta families. Ones Ah can find anyway."

"Understood and good thinking."

Moira stretched an hour later, dirt packed onto the most recent grave in the snow and dirt. Captain Hunter carefully lifted another long plank but found nothing underneath except a torn crumple of sailcloth and stiff with the cold. Moira looked around; they had only managed to search a quarter of the wreckage so far.

"Cap'n, Ah be thinkin'. We may be goin' about this all wrong."

Hunter stood and stretched his own knotted muscles. "Go on."
"We be lookin' fer tracks o' survivors. In this snow? Ah be thinkin' that
if Ah be in a bird goin' down, especially on her bow, where would Ah
want tae be? Ah'd think near the boilers."

Hunter looked at the whole of the wreckage. The bow, or front
of the ship, was in several large pieces near one another. The stern or
rear of the ship typically held passenger and officer quarters as well as
the airship's tiny engine room underneath both for boilers and batteries.
That entire section lay partially buried in the snow but was largely
intact. The reinforced plates of wood and copper protected the stern,
not from a boiler explosion but from impact on a snow-covered
mountainside.

"Moira, I think I owe you an ale. Brilliant!"

In two steps Hunter put himself in earshot of the other two
searchers. "O'Fallon! William! The boiler room!"

O'Fallon waved a hand in reply and motioned his younger
partner. By the time Hunter and Moira reached the ruined stern section,
the other two had used steel rods from nearby to pry open a bent copper
and steel door that led below. Their footsteps squeaked in the powdery
snow, Moira and Hunter climbed aboard the wreck and joined in. The
snow fell harder, the cold hampering the work. Finally, with the added
help, the door relinquished its hold on the frame. With a groan and a
sharp pop that echoed in the cold air, the door was swung aside and fell
in a lopsided heap next to them. A brief cloud of powdery snow
surrounded them for a moment. William let out a heavy sigh, gestured
to the black doorway and grinned.

"Your doorway Cap'n."

Moira waved a hand at William. "Sush a moment boy." Suddenly, her eyes went wide at a sound so faint, she barely could made it out. From the darkness, the hollow ring of copper being struck with something metal reached their ears. Behind that was muffled and panic filled shouts. In a mad dash, she grabbed the door frame and dropped from sight into the musty darkness below.

"What's she on about?" William asked in surprise. Hunter and O'Fallon exchanged a look. Captain Hunter shrugged.

"Moira's hearing is quite good."

O'Fallon started to reply with some story as an example when Moira's voice piped up from below.

"Cap'n! We got a couple here!"

O'Fallon stopped his story before it started and shrugged.

Hunter grinned at the two crewmen with him. "Never fails, somehow she hears them. Well you lads heard the lady, let's lend her a hand."

With William and O'Fallon helping, a moment later two children, a boy and girl no more than six and nine years of age respectfully, emerged into the light.

Chapter 3

"That's all Cap'n. The rest down here didn't hold out." Moira called from below deck.

Hunter sighed and turned to the two children who were bundled in a blanket William had carried.

"Well met young sirrah and lady, we've got warm food and clothes ... "

His welcome faded on his lips as the sound of a hiss and whine of steam powered propellers echoed in the air.

O'Fallon, hearing it too, stopped partway out of the hatch, "Steambats? What be they doin' here?"

Just then the pair of steam-powered biplanes, named 'Steambats' for the bat shape to the quartet of wings attached to each aircraft, arced gracefully to the right in a turn above the wreck. The cloth and wooden fuselage with its brass fittings had been painted a deep blue, long since faded from exposure to the sun and weather. Before anyone could become comfortable with their new airborne visitors, both of the nimble aircraft turned sharply and dove. Their angle of attack was directly towards where Hunter, O'Fallon, Moira, William and the children were at that moment.

"Down!" Moira shouted before ducking below deck.

A moment later the whine of steambat engines turned to an angry buzz. From two long nozzles attached to hoses on the wings erupted blue white bolts of lighting, guided by streams of high pressure water jets. The electrified stream scoured the deck and snow, tearing a pair of lines into whatever they touched. Nearly singed in the process, Captain Hunter threw himself across the children to protect them. Bits of wood and brass exploded from the wreck and rained down in all directions. Snow vaporized in whitish clouds of fog before it condensed back to snow. Finally the biplanes tore by overhead, passed beyond the wreck and climbed above the trees towards the clouds again.

Hunter eased up slowly, taking deep breaths to steady his voice. He had been shot at countless times when he served in the Royal Navy, but one never grew used to such an experience. Adrenaline tempered his nerves, and after a second breath he looked down at the terrified children.

"Both ok?"

He was rewarded by a pair of nodding, grimy faces drawn with lines of hunger and fear. From the hatch, William's panic-white face peered over the edge and looked skyward. Behind him, O'Fallon had already drawn a pistol and true to his nature, looked for a chance to soothe his anger. Moira however, was not within sight.

"Good, now a brief introduction. I'm Captain Anthony Hunter of the *Brass Griffin* and this is my crew. We're here to help."

Immediately, the children screamed again. Quickly sitting up, Hunter turned to see a the steambats complete a turn for another attack run, guns crackling with lightning held in check. Instinctively he scanned the sky but saw no sight of the *Griffin*. Without a word, mouth set in a hard frown, Hunter scooped up the children in his arms and raced for the rock outcrop that had helped with the demise of the *Marie Celeste*.

Bits of wood and other debris from the wreck exploded behind the Captain. Throwing himself forward, he skid across the mud and snow until he came to a rest beneath the protection of the rock shelter with his two charges. The buzz of propellers surged by overhead then grew dim as the two aircraft returned to the thick clouds.

"Hush crying now, it'll be fine. Just fine now. Now who are you two, eh?"

Dressed in a modest blue-gray dress, black vest with white lace trim that was now stained with black smudges of soot, she still looked very much a young lady from a family of means. The younger boy with her was dressed similarly, in brown knee-length trousers, brown jacket and a cream colored shirt, all stained similarly like the girl. The young lady rubbed her nose with the back of her hand and found her voice first.

"I'm Angela Von Patterson, he's my brother Miles."

Hunter smiled, "Well good to meet you both. I know your Uncle, he hired myself and my crew to come looking for you."

Angela looked at Hunter with large eyes, "He did?"

"Yes young miss, he did."

"Captain! Ye breathin'?" Came a woman's shout from the wreck.

"Hale and whole, Moira, by the outcropping."

A hurried crunch of footsteps in snow, then Moira, William and O'Fallon dove behind the rocks as well. William tossed a half-filled, grimy bag into the snow.

"Grabbed a few trinkets from below decks. Never know when somethin' might come in handy. If they come back," William gestured towards the cloudy, gray sky overhead. "What were they wantin' anyways, Cap'n?"

Hunter cast an apprehensive glance overhead. "I daresay have no idea. It could have been a band of raiders who happened upon the wreck and thought searching it would be simpler with no survivors. Perhaps smugglers who frequent the area. If luck is with us, they won't be a concern either way. O'Falllon, wind that opti-telegraphic of yours and see if the *Griffin* is paying attention."

"Aye, Cap'n."

From his belt pouch, O'Fallon removed a rectangular brass box slightly longer than eight inches on the long side by four inches. Pushing a brass rivet, a small wood and brass 'S' shaped handle extended from the side with a pop sound. O'Fallon cranked the handle with a few quick turns until a pair of lights glowed dimly on the faceplate. Below the lights, O'Fallon opened a small panel. Using the few undersized typewriter keys there he tapped out a hailing message.

"If they be sailin' within range, Cap'n, they'll answer."

"*Griffin* here. Anyone found?"

"Be findin' two an' then some. There be a pair o' steambats takin' bites at us, can ye be takin' a swat at 'em?"

"Been in a scrape also, as soon as we patch a few holes we'll be underway to your location."

The four of them exchanged a look, O'Fallon keyed the device again. "Say again *Griffin?*"

Suddenly a bullet ripped the opti-telegraphic from O'Fallon's hand. The device showered a bright flash of sparks and electricity before it pitched into the snow. Miles and Angela screamed and huddled close while the crew drew weapons with an eye to the rocks above.

"Where?" Hunter growled while William eased himself over to the children and spoke quietly to try and ease their terror.

In answer, a hail of bullets hammered the rocks around them. Chips and splinters of gravel rained down and flew past their faces. Through the chaos, Moira spotted figures just over seventy yards off and upwards among the rocks. With no time to speak, she aimed her long-barreled Army Colt and fired, sending a .44 caliber round towards the rocks. Quickly, the others followed her lead with the sharp explosions of gunfire. In seconds the firefight stopped with acrid gun smoke filling the air.

William looked up and around carefully, "Them 'bats still there?"

Moira waved him quiet then nodded over the faint sounds of stumbling in the packed snow. "They be off findin' a place ta lick their wounds. So, they're gone for now. The thing that makes me itch be that they found us here. How'd they be knowin'? Them fliers haven't had the time to set down anywhere."

Hunter opened the cylinder to reload his revolver, "I was pondering that also. They had to have been waiting, which means we were set up for some reason." He dropped the last bullet in and clicked the cylinder shut. "We'll find out who that was soon enough, once we're back aboard the *Griffin*."

William voice shook slightly and the two children sobbing caught the captain's ears. "Cap'n ..." was all he managed.
A few feet from William, lay O'Fallon face down. A stain of red slowly pooled beneath him in the snow.

Hunter swore softly under his breath. "William, get your medical bag, we need to bandage him before we can get him to shelter and us away from here."

William nodded grimly, yet still speechless, and withdrew a small leather wrapped parcel from his shoulder bag before he got to work.

Chapter 4

Krumer Whitehorse, first mate of the *Brass Griffin*, slammed a calloused fist against the rough-hewn table below deck. The opti-telegraphic on the table shuddered from the vibration, rattling its mainspring and battery connection. As if in protest, the brass plated device sparked and shuddered before its faceplate lights grew dim. "O'Fallon? O'Fallon!"

Tonks Wilkerson, the broad-shouldered pilot of the *Brass Griffin* with his distinctive thin face and hawk-like nose, put a firm hand on the first mate's shoulder. "Don't care a whit if ya are an orc or that Cap'n Hunter left ya in charge with him groundside. Yellin' and beatin' it won't do ya much good. It's got a short in the thing and ya know it."

"Something's wrong, I can feel it, Tonks."
Tonks hefted the brass box and experimentally turned the 'S' shaped crank on the side. "Mainspring's still good. Looks like it and a battery wire's gone and got loose. I'll pry it open and see if I can get it tightened down." Tonks glanced at Krumer's deepening frown. "Ya know the four o' 'em been around more'n once."

"I do."

"Alright. We only took some glancing shots broadsides from that pirate or whoever they were. The starboard lightning net can't be deployed until we get back ta a port for serious repairs and one boiler's leaking more than normal. Fortunately, we didn't go an' lose anybody ta the broadside we took and we're still mostly maneuverable. It's just we're not gonna be fast about it." The young man scratched the brownish stubble on his chin and walked up the the ladder to the deck above. The sounds of cutting, sawing and other signs of repair were thick in the air along with fumes of tar, hemp rope and sawdust. Tonks emerged mid deck and shouted among the scurry of activity. "Come about and watch her trim, those bow lines are still frayin'."

Tonks stepped aside then glanced back over his shoulder when Krumer emerged from below. "Setting course, Mr Whitehorse. Hope there's no rough reception waitin'."

Krumer sighed and glanced out across the billowing clouds, white and fluffy like so much mist on a cold winter's day. The *Griffin* was higher up than before. She rode the top of the clouds that partially obscured the mountainside below, not to mention any usual flight path of other airships. In the distance he saw the tan, double bat shaped wings and box girders of two steambat aircraft dart up and through the gray and white clouds of a low cloud bank. When the aircraft vanished, his frowned returned.

"As do I, Mr. Wilkerson. Spirit's willing."

Chapter 5

A small fire fueled by a pyramid of cut branches burned bright in the shallow fire. Heat warmed a small tin pot of water held precariously above it by a crude stand. Outward from the pit, a few blankets were laid out just in the glow of the fire. Shadows from those danced against the dried remains of an ancient, overturned maple tree. Near the fire, Captain Hunter dropped a small pile of branches just outside the fire's reach. He then watched in silence while William checked the bandages on O'Fallon's head and right thigh. The quartermaster opened his eyes and managed a weak smile.

"Nae worry Cap'n, be takin' more'n this tae lay me low."
A thin smile played across Hunter's face while he reached for a tin cup and a small bag of dried, brown leaves. "Get some rest my friend. Drink that tea William's made, it'll help you sleep."

Carefully pouring the scalding water from the pot, Hunter mixed it with leaves for his own tea. Returning the pot to the fire, he rose and walked to the edge of the camp. He watched the evening moonlight play across the snow-draped pines. Gently, the wind picked up and a light snow drifted again from the scattered clouds. The forest was moderately thick here and the shadows cast by the moonlight moved ever so slightly. In the distance, a sharp howl from a wolf hunting in the distance echoed in the night air. From behind, a crunch of snow heralded Moira's approach. She paused next to Hunter and tugged her long coat around her a bit tighter.

"Bugger me, it be cold. How long do ya think we 'ave Cap'n?"

"A few hours at the least. A day at most. This snow and the whipping we gave them at the crash should slow any pursuit down a touch."

"It be all disturbin' if ya ask me. Comin' outta nowhere like that, they had ta been layin' in wait. Think they were usin' the wee ones as bait?"

Hunter turned that over in his mind, sparing a glance at the two children. William had bundled them up in spare blankets. Angela and Miles huddled together for warmth and reassurance, occupying the space between the overturned tree and the small campfire. It provided the warmest place, for heat from the fire reflected back from the overturned roots.

"Bait? I couldn't imagine why they'd be bait for us. No, I suspect we led them to the children unknowingly." Hunter took a sip of the tea and offered the cup to Moira without a word.

"Thankee, I could use a cuppa." Moira took a sip of the hot drink and handed it back. "Followin' or waitin', shame on it either way. It brings ta mind dark reasons why."

"I wish I could think otherwise, but it was too convenient. They arrived the moment we brought those two children out of that wreck, something like that isn't happenstance, my dear."

She nodded slightly in agreement. After a moment's

consideration she added, "Or we be in a bad bargain."

"Spot on point. I had not thought of that. However, if that's so, I can't figure what their Uncle Ian would get from it since he hired us to find them." Light flakes of snow drifted in the wind to brush his face while he looked up to the cloudy sky. He sighed, exasperation and fatigue taking its toll. "Either way it's something to sleep on. For tonight we'll need watches."

"Aye Cap'n. Ah'll take first light."

"Well and done, Moira. William?"

William looked up from where he sat mending a small hole in a spare blanket. "Aye Cap'n?"

"Setting watches between the three of us. Moira has first light. What say you? We've quite a lot of night to cover."

"Now's fine for me Cap'n. Ya can get some sleep. O'Fallon's only just drifted off a bit ago, I kin watch him for awhile. 'Sides, I been needin' ta mend ma blanket for awhile."

"Fair enough," Hunter yawned despite his best efforts to resist it. Methodically, he reached down to wind the mainspring of his clockwork right hand. Carefully he flexed it, the interlocking gears within the chocolate brown rhino-hide leather joints protested at the cold. Hunter winced as the temperature and sensation of the cold gears radiated subtly through his arm. "Watch close, we'll break camp at first light."

The wolf's howl broke the night air again. The trio cast glances into the dark trees around them. Hunter frowned.

"And by all means, eyes sharp tonight. I don't think we're

alone."

Embers glowed in the coals of the fire struggling against the chill the next morning. A dusting of light snow added to the effect, blanketing the camp and everyone in it with a touch of frost. Moira cupped her hands near her mouth and blew. Fog from her breath encircled her head while she walked between the lumps of blankets and coats, rousing the campsite.

Captain Hunter rubbed his eyes and yawned. "Any signs?"

"A bit o' smoke near the ridge. No signs o' the fliers."

"Good, with luck we'll put some distance between us and them." Hunter stood and stretched. A bit more alert against the morning light, he knelt and recovered his blanket. Carefully he knocked the light snow from it and rolled it tight.

Moira, having already packed her blanket, walked over to the two smaller bundles of blankets on the far side of the coals. "Up to it. Let's pack up so's we kin be movin' downslope."

"We gotta?" Came the little boy's whimpering reply.

"Aye that ya do, young sirrah."

While the children rose, stiff and irritable, William stood with a yawning stretch then checked the quartermaster near him. O'Fallon's eyes opened slowly. "Where be we t'day?"

"Same as day afore. Let's check them bandages."
Despite the cold of the snowy mountain air, Hunter stepped a few paces away from the campsite into the tree line. Carefully, he scanned the ridge behind and above them. Just beyond the rocks a thin column of gray smoke, barely visible, rose into the morning air. His thoughts

turned over the possibilities in his mind. Some concerned themselves with the immediate necessity of a morning meal, while others were not so pleasant. Namely why their attackers were being so relentless.

"Cap'n?"

Hunter's eyes never left the ridge line. "Yes, Mr. Falke?"

"About packed and ready and ... Cap'n? We've had some company."

Something in the young man's tone struck Hunter as off. In the few years since William had joined his crew, William Falke had displayed a knack for finding the unusual. This time was no exception.

There in the snow, the young man pointed out the light depression of a pair of tracks.

"That's a paw print, oddly shaped though. One too many toes for a wolf or cat. The other I've never seen. Where do these go? Have you trailed them?"

"Only some Cap'n. Picked 'em up outside camp, I did. The big tracks came not far away, watched us a bit then left in a hurry."

"The other?"

"Chasin' the first I 'spect. Big cat or wolf. Just can't figure where'd it come from, though. It kept climbin' trees then jumpin' down. Its almost like it was around the camp watchin' us the whole time."

"That's not a comforting thought. Next time we need to check the tree canopy. We were lucky this time. Had that animal chose, it could've jumped in camp and hurt any of us."

"Sorry Cap'n."

"No harm done, I never considered it myself, either. Let's return to camp before our friends above the ridge there get the idea to take a walk."

"Aye Cap'n."

Chapter 6

Tonks stood near the starboard railing and watched while four crewmen turned the longskiff loading winches. Suddenly, one of the ropes pulled at a sharper angle than the other four, threatening to snap. The pilot leaned over the rail. Below, the longskiff used by Captain Hunter and his landing party the day before hovered just inside the leather loading harness. The harness was the typical kind, being a wide net of leather straps used to help maneuver such a craft aboard larger vessels, such as the *Griffin*. The ropes from on deck wound their way up through pulleys and over to the harness itself that cradled the unharmed longskiff. The only two crewman aboard the smaller airship were busy with slowly releasing the air from the longskiff's gas bag. The small propellers on the craft, however, turned far too quickly than they should.

"More slack in your bag! Cut your engine or you'll snap the moorin' lines!"

"Aye!" Came the reply from crew aboard the longskiff.

"Problem, Mr. Wilkerson?"

Tonks turned to see Krumer Whitehorse approach. "Nay anythin' that some closer attention would cover, sir."

"Understood. Anything found aboard the 'skiff?'"

"Some lads went through it close. Blankets and a few supplies are missing, but not all the travel packs are gone. No sign of the landing party yet. The wreck's a mess though, and they found gunshot and other sign of a fight. Got some scourin' that now, maybe make some sense of it."

Krumer nodded, his jaw set, his mouth in a hard line of concern. He folded his arms over his chest then tapped a finger idly on one of his short tusks. "Did they find any idea who did the attacking? Same group as found us?"

"Hard ta say. Plenty of damage from the same kind 'a ordinance that they were usin' on us. Lightning guns and all that. They'll send word when they find somethin' or if somethin' finds them."

Krumer paused in thought, watching the crew slowly haul the longskiff aboard. He let his eyes play over the craft from its partially deflated gas bag to snow-covered skids and undamaged hull. "Just the blankets are gone, might mean they are camped nearby."

"We kept spotters through the night, but none claimed ta see campfire. A'course the treeline's thicker downslope. If they headed that way, we might've missed them."

Krumer swore under his breath a moment. "All of this. This cannot be just coincidence. If those were pirates that happened across us, that longskiff would be missing anything not nailed down."

"Aye, true that. Searchers I've got down there had sent word about the lightning gunfire. It was all about on ground, trees and what's left of the *Marie Celeste*. Krumer, we're bein' hunted. Ya know it, as do

I. I just can't tell who they're gunnin' for."

"Also, if they were hunting us, why here? Why now? This isn't the most well-traveled flight path for most ships. Cargo ships take the more southern route. News of the *Celeste* going down wasn't known when when we set out this way. How did these pirates find us or this place?"

Tonks looked stunned. "Yer not claimin' a spy aboard? Can't be, we've not taken on crew in better on two years, no one'd be disloyal here."

Krumer shook his head. "I'm not saying a spy. Like you just said, it couldn't be. We're a small ship and a tight crew. We all know each other too well. I'm wondering what we took aboard. Maybe something in our supplies or any cargo?"

The pilot frowned. "We've got a tracker on us."

"I think so. Worst case, the more elaborate ones can pick up sound like an opti-telegraphic, but they would have to be nearly as large also. Spread the word, but do it quietly. Search the ship. Something's aboard with us and we need to find it."

Tonks nodded with a frown. "Aye ta that."

Word spread quietly, yet quickly among the nearly twenty crew members aboard. Immediately all bent themselves to the task. Repairing the damage the *Brass Griffin* had sustained was important. Making sure they were not being hunted like a rabbit was more so. The more common areas such as the main deck, midship area below decks for meals and crew storage, the hold and so on were searched more than once. Each man and woman took to searching their belongings and sleeping hammock - or cabin in the case of Krumer and Tonks -on their own. Searchers even prowled through the various places for lookouts to stand watch on the bow or above on the gas bag.

An hour later, the search had uncovered little more than frustration and a growing anxiety that they may be attacked again. Only this time, they would not be fully prepared to withstand it. In the small, plain cabin that served as a common room for the captain and the *Griffin*'s officers' quarters, Tonks lifted a long wooden case that held the bundle of navigational charts for the ship. He flipped the latch open and dumped the contents unceremoniously on the small wooden table in the room. Parchment charts fell out, some partially unrolling. He shook the box twice then, convinced it was empty, set it on the table with a sigh of frustration. Most of the ship had been searched thoroughly, some places twice over and no one had anything to show for it.

Krumer walked out of his cabin with an expression similar to that Tonks wore. "Anything?"

"Nay a bloody thing. Krumer. If there's one ta be had, its hidden tight."

"Or worse yet, hiddin on the landing party." Krumer's rising frustration was readily apparent in his voice now. "Which if it is, we cannot contact them and warn them! I cannot believe …"

Tonks waved a hand at his friend. "Hush, now. Wait. Didya hear that?"

Krumer bottled his temper and frowned in concentration.

"Hear what? I don't …"

Then he stopped in mid-sentence when a faint, fleeting buzz reached his ears.

Tonks nodded, a smile of satisfaction slowly grew on his face. "I'm hearin' it too."

Slowly, carefully, the pair turned to face different parts of the room. They each listened, and when they heard the faint buzz again, took a careful step in that direction. In no time, they found themselves staring at a blank corner. Krumer looked to Tonks quizzically. Tonks shrugged, a little confused himself. Then an idea struck him, the narrow cabinets high on the wall to his right could hold the source of the sound. He gestured at them and reached for the knob of the closet cabinet. As if on cue, they heard the buzz again from behind the cabinet door.

Tonks smiled as Krumer tensed to grab whatever the source of the sound was. The pilot took a slow breath. If the device could fit in a small cabinet it would have to be small. Perhaps no larger than a person's open palm. Especially given that cabinet was only used to store spare twine and cotton rags for cleaning. He had dealt with such items in the past when he worked for the Foreign Service. Never had he expected to see them again, especially here. He yanked open the cabinet door.

Immediately a small object shrieked in alarm and shot out of a dark space beside a stack of cotton cloths. A glint of brass among the blur was all they saw as it raced around the room.

Krumer dove immediately for it but crashed into the wall. His hands clutched at air where it had been. "Missed!"

Tonks watched the small brass blur fly about the room as it

looked for an opening to escape. "Ya can't grab at it like that, it'll expect that. We can't let it outta our sight, though. We'll lose it for sure."

"How do we catch it then?"

A thought came to the pilot. "Burlap! Them stacks of old coffee bags we've got from the last cargo we hauled. Catch it with that or some other kinda cloth. Like catchin' fish with a net."

Krumer got to his feet and raced out of the cabin, calling for the crew. Tonks eyed the blur with an impish grin. "Oh you're wantin' loose, I can tell it. Well, we're not gonna hurt ya, but we gotta know what ya know or who ya workin' for."

The little blur darted this way and that, Tonks did his best to jump in the way to block it, but in the end it outmaneuvered him. It raced out out the cabin door. "It's on deck!" Tonks shouted, fast in pursuit of it.

Above, the crew scrambled with old brown burlap bags stamped with either plantation names or simply 'coffee' on them. They swatted and waved at the blur but none could catch it. They managed to barely prevent it from flying off ship. Finally, the brass blur dodged one crewman, sailed beneath Krumer's legs and soared upward towards the gas bag and rigging.

"Don't let it leave the ship!" Krumer shouted in a mix of anger and disbelief.

Suddenly a shirtless Tonks Wilkerson threw himself from the rigging directly at the blur. Man and flying object collided in mid air. No sooner than that, Tonks wrapped his shirt around the buzzing creature like he would bag a bird. Just as he finished, he and his captive fell to the wooden deck sideways in a hard landing. He held the shirt closed tight, inside his captive struggled fiercely. Finally, the struggles and angry buzzing subsided. The pilot carefully unwrapped part of his catch.

In his shirt was a brass dragonfly, no longer than ten inches in length and an inch and a half wide at its thickest point. Its wings were a gossamer, copper metal mesh and its body a series of brass tubes jointed with some unusual gray leather. The teardrop-shaped head with its ruby faceted eyes looked at Tonks then around at the crew nervously.

Tonks stood slowly, careful not to harm his small captive. "Mr Whitehorse. Looks like ya were right. We've been bugged."

"Good work Mr. Wilkerson. Can we learn anything from it?"

The pilot raised an eyebrow at the brass dragonfly with a grin. "More'n a bit I'd suspect. Depends on how helpful it'll be. Now little bug, just so yer on the same terms I am, all we want ta know is what yer doin' here and who sent ya. No harms comin' to ya. Understand?"

After a moment of consideration, the brass dragonfly nodded slowly, nervously and buzzed once.

Chapter 7

The group broke camp just past dawn after a quiet meal of jerked beef, dried fruit and a three-inch-round barley biscuits still referred to by its ancient name, 'salschoon'. Morning wore into mid-day while the knots of gray clouds that had lasted since morning slowly made way for pale streams of daylight. Following a game trail William discovered, the group descended, leaving the trees behind for a wide clearing. There, snow lay in thick drifts of white powder on the ground and pine trees that dotted the gentle slope. Despite events of the previous day, spirits rose just as the sun reached its zenith at noon.

William, having taken his turn carrying young Miles and a pack of blankets, stepped around a snowdrift that had mingled with a large rock. He shifted the pack and the boy's weight on his shoulders and scanned the sky. "Anybody else hearin' that?"

Moira helped Angela over a patch of ice hidden by snow. Once she set the girl onto ground next to her she looked up quizzically. "What sound be that?"

Captain Hunter, who was pulling O'Fallon on a crude litter, paused and frowned in concentration.

William looked up and around again. "The hum. Thought it

'twere a bird, y'know? Like one o' them hummin'birds I heard of."

Hunter shook his head. "Too cold for that here. They'll be in the warmer lands."

Angela looked up. "I hear it, too."

Just as the sound reached Moira and Hunter's ears, Moira shot Hunter an alarmed look then gestured to a pair of dark shapes far overhead. "That's nae bird. Less they come with steam engines and two wings, mind ya."

Hunter snarled. "Steambats! Make for the trees!"

The powdery snow fought the group as they staggered for the trees only yards away. Above, a pair of steambats hummed overhead like a pair of giant bees. Breaking the clouds, they passed over once, banked, then dove for the running figures like wolves to hunt. Bullets screamed. Streams of water-guided lightning crackled. Snow sprayed in great white plumes behind the group, drawing closer with every step. Moira, with Angela in her arms, reached the thick stand of trees first. Depositing the young girl behind a tree, she spun and knelt in one smooth motion, pistols in hand. Steadily, she aimed while the plumes of snow and the hail of bullets clawed at the heels of her crewmates. William tripped on a hidden branch, Miles spilled with a scream of terror into the snow.

Without a glance back, William grabbed Miles and threw himself at the trees, falling on a patch of packed snow. They slid breakneck towards the forest. Further behind, Hunter dropped the litter and bodily drug O'Fallon to his feet. Hauling the quartermaster over his shoulders, the captain struggled in the deep snow, racing for his life while the bullets peppered the ground inches behind him.

Moira took a deep breath to steady her aim. Overhead the steambat drifted left, then right like a bird caught on the wind. She waited, letting the shouts around her and bark of gunfire fall away. Suddenly the small silhouette of the closest aircraft's pilot crossed her gunsight. She smiled a wicked grin much the way a she-wolf snarls over prey and whispered, "Gotcha."

Her pistols bucked twice. Time slowed for the sliver of a heartbeat. Two shots arced up and out of the trees along the path the attacking aircraft's own gunfire had taken. Three seconds later, time collapsed on itself. The pilot jerked once then twice. His steambat sprayed steam and heated water in a wide shower over the clearing before it banked wildly to the right. The second aircraft, caught off guard, narrowly avoided collision with his wounded comrade. He pulled up and over the damaged aircraft then banked to the left, which ruined any chance at a better shot at the people below.

The wounded aircraft danced on the wind, fighting the pilot's attempt to regain control. Finally, the craft leveled out and gently turned around, heading back up the slope in the direction it had come. Behind it, a plume of steam traced its retreat.

Hunter slowly eased O'Fallon down behind a tree and gulped in the crisp mountain air. O'Fallon looked pale but conscious.

"We be all here? Sound off!" Croaked the quartermaster.

Moira closed her eyes quietly a moment to steady her nerves, then she dropped her pistols into their holsers. She spared a smile to Angela and gave the girl a reassuring hug.

Angela fought back a terrified, angry sob while Moira called over her shoulder. "Moira's here and I've the young miss with me."

"Miles and Sirrah William," was a small, shaken, piped reply from behind a tree. That was followed by a deeper voice that finished the call with a wheeze of, "Aye. We're hale and whole."

Hunter limped a step or two and sat next to O'Fallon, "Aye, I'm here as well as any."

"At least we be all breathin'." O'Fallon turned slightly to look up at the sky and the remaining steambat that circled far overhead. He turned back and leaned against the rough bark of the tree, eyes closed while he fought back a stab of pain.

Moira tossed her pack on he ground and dug out a blanket which she promptly fashioned a crude shawl for the young girl. "Darlin' yer chilled. Ya shoulda' said somethin'."

Angela, pale from the cold, fought another shudder. "I ... I'm alright. I'm more worried about Miles."

Moira smiled. "Well yer a good sister at that, though. William! Get yer lazy backside up!"

A small struggle ensued, but William emerged from the tangle of blankets and bags that threatened to bury him. Miles helped his friend with tossing a few blankets aside as well. "Aye ... just sortin' y'know?"

The shawl finished, a growl resounded in Moira's voice. "I'd just want ta be knowin' who the bloody buggers are!"

Hunter exhaled a light cloud of breath. "I don't know." He looked over at young Miles, who was fully engrossed in helping William sort and repack the spilled blankets. The captain looked over at Angela in turn, bundled in her makeshift shawl. She was speaking to

Moira shyly, much as any child being overly-doted on would.

"I simply just do not know." The captain repeated firmly in frustration. "What I do know is once we reach a village or somewhere with more shelter than a few trees, we can take a hand at repairing the opti-telegraphic and call the *Griffin*. Then perhaps pay these thugs back in kind."

O'Fallon nodded slowly, careful of his head wound. "Aye tae that. Krumer'll be stayin' till past all the ship's stores run dry." He looked up at the remaining steambat that circled high above. "What be he doin' up there?"

"Waiting for us to emerge from the trees, I'd likely imagine. He can't stay aloft all day. A craft that size doesn't have the fuel for that small a steam engine."

While the two men watched, the craft dipped its wings once, twice, then gently banked to the right.

O'Fallon frowned while he tried to guess the pilot's intent. "Now what be he on about?"

In answer, a plume of white snow blossomed on the higher slopes of the mountain as a dull rumble of thunder growled in the distance.

"Light's breath!" Hunter exclaimed.

"Avalanche!"

Ignoring their discarded packs, William hefted Miles and took the lead, crashing through the snow and dodging trees. Behind him ran Moira and Angela, then further back, Captain Hunter with O'Fallon. From up slope the white plume gave way to a curling wave of snow. At first it was a slow ripple along the mountainside, but in seconds it was a wall of ice, rock and snow several stories tall.

The group raced downhill, shoving through ankle-deep snow. Thick, low-hanging boughs tore at their clothes, slowing them down while the deluge of snow and rocks roared closer behind them. William slid to a stop and pointed as young Miles collided into him in the rush.

"Cap'n! There!"

Off to William's right sat a cluster of ancient rocks that towered fifteen feet above. Caught in a depression in the ground, they stood tilted at a wide angle against each other. Most important, they were shelter. Hunter nodded once in appreciation then bellowed to be heard over the roar of the oncoming landslide.

"To the rocks!"

William and Miles reached the small cave first as the spray of snow pushed into the trees. Moira and Angela stumbled along moments later. Lagging behind were Captain Hunter and O'Fallon. Trees bent and snapped from the press of the avalanche, snow flying thick in the air like an icy waterfall. As O'Fallon stumbled on a tree root, both himself and Hunter fell in a heap into the snow. Moira instantly raced out into the impending maelstrom. William yelled but the deafening roar muffled his cries.

Pitched face-first into the ground, Hunter raised his head when the wall of ice and death arrived, hammering him down like a giant fist as snow and rocks swirled deadly through the air. Stunned, his vision blurred from each rock, each branch that hit him. Pain lanced through him but soon it gave way to a cold darkness that tried to blanket him. Dimly, he heard William shout in surprise and Moira exclaim something in shock. Before the darkness swallowed him, he felt one last abrupt tug on his coat. Through the storm of snow, a short mass of brown fur had grabbed Hunter in a pair of strong claws and pulled.

Chapter 8

Silence and darkness shrouded the cave while outside, the sounds of the avalanche dimmed to nothing. Seconds passed slowly, then sounds of life stirred in the complete darkness. Survivors moved cautiously, feeling their way along rough stone to make sense of their new surroundings.

William coughed at dust that lingered in the air. "Anyone be thinkin' ta drag a light along?"
Moira sat up slowly, careful to not bump into what she could not see. "Ah box of tindersticks and a striker, hold on."

The blacksmith fumbled with cold fingers at a small pouch on her belt. By only touch, she withdrew a small leather bundle of sticks and a flat, thumb-sized piece of slate. Slowly, she worked one of the tindersticks out of the bundle. Then she struck the treated end of the tinderstick against the slate once, then twice.

One small spark followed another, then the end of the tinderstick burst into flame. Moira held the burning stick high to let the feeble light shine as best it could. The cave was small, but could just accommodate the group. The only entrance had been completely filled with snow. At the back of a cave a small niche rose upwards into the rock.

Her tinderstick's glow also revealed grim and tired faces of people she expected to see, and a few things she did not. Namely, a small discarded pile of branches, some with leaves still attached. They were not much, but would make for a simple, yet serviceable source of heat. Moira laid hands upon one and ran the tinderstick over it until the flame caught onto the leaves and branch itself.

"We gotta lot o' diggin' ahead o' us." William sighed with a mournful look at the cave entrance.

Captain Hunter, however, was not looking at the snow. He had fixed a stern look on one of their number. "That we do, but once we are free of our little burrow, I, for one, will want a explanation, Miss Angela, straight away."

There in the dim shadows of the cavern, Angela sat crouched against the wall. Her clothes were torn with bits of fur thrust through the ripped holes. All-too-human eyes peered out from an obvious canine face, complete with a wolf's snout. Distinctive wolf-like ears had thrust through her hair, and while her body retained much of her human appearance, her hands had developed small claws. Her feet had a definite canine curve to her legs that ended in large paws.

Lithe as a panther, Angela shifted her weight uneasily. Aware of the uncomfortable stares from her companions, the look of worried concern from her younger brother, and the hard look of Captain Hunter made her more self-conscious than a girl her age would normally be. Her eyes drifted uneasily around the group to rest on Hunter. She nodded, almost ashamed.

"Yes Sirrah Captain. I'll explain then."

"Don't you hurt her!" Blurted Miles in a fit of tears and young rage, his small arms shaking with all the bound energy of an upset youth.

William put his hands on the boy's shoulders. "Hush now, lad. No way to talk to the Cap'n."

"He's not my Captain! He's not our father or anyone!"
Hunter sighed, his look softening a touch. "No boy, I'm not. But I and my crew were charged to bring you both back safely and that's what we plan to do. Secrets like this? Right now lad, I've got to say aren't helpful. However, that's neither here nor there. This snow won't dig itself. Angela, Moira, help me dig. William, see if that niche in back of the cave leads anywhere."

"What ... what a' me?" Miles stammered.

"Think on what I've said, lad. Think hard on it and sit with O'Fallon. He'll be needing someone with him right now. If there's anything else we don't know, and you think we ought to, speak up." Miles turned a faint shade of pink and obeyed with a downcast look on his face. He sat next to O'Fallon and stared glumly at the dirt-strewn cave floor.

The group worked in silence, as much to conserve air as it was their conversation had lost its momentum. After a few minutes William returned from his exploration to shake his head slowly.

"Can't tell where that chimney's goin'. No wider than my own fist could be fittin'. Seems taller than twice my height though, so I'm not thinkin' the younglings could be scootin' through it."
Hunter shook his cold hands to try and warm them from digging at the snow, then sighed with a faint hint of frustration over the news.

"Unfortunate. Well, another pair of hands working to clear the snow won't hurt."

Working in shifts, the group labored in silence. They scooped at a steady pace, depositing the snow in the back of the cave. Two hours later, hands numb from the cold, William broke the surface of the snow.

"Ah'm through!"

With an elated grin and renewed vigor, William desperately shoved the snow aside to scramble up. He emerged with a deep breath of relief, and smiled. Warm afternoon sunlight played through the trees overhead and lifted the chill just slightly in the mountain air. The young sailor closed his eyes and took another deep breath, enjoying the immediate relief from the claustrophobic cave below. Having enjoyed his brief moment of sunlight, he slowly opened his eyes, then froze in shock. There, no more than two yards from where he stood, was a large furred creature that had just stepped from behind a tree. Covered in white, matted fur from head to toe, the six-foot-tall beast took a heavy breath and a step closer, leaving the same peculiar animal tracks William had seen outside the camp the night before.

William tried to duck back down the tunnel, but realized too late it was not wide enough for that. In his haste, the snow had fallen back in around his waist, and he was stuck. Digging away at the snow at his waist, he only caused more to fall in around him. Suddenly the beast grunted and charged. Ten yards distance between them became five, then one. William went pale and tried to yell but his voice caught in his throat. When the beast was nearly on him, he managed to croak out a strangled alarm.

"Cap'n! We got Comp'ny!"

Chapter 9

Hunter had turned at William's shout just as the crewman's kicking legs were jerked abruptly upwards, out of sight. Immediately, Angela snarled and leapt towards the tunnel.

"Angela! No!" Hunter reached for her, but the young werewolf was too quick. She was up and above before he could lay hand to her. He yanked his pistol from the holster at his belt.

"Bloody hell of a thing."

Moira, in turn, drew weapons. O'Fallon even struggled to rise despite protests from young Miles.

Hunter shook his head. "We can't all rush out there."

Moira quickly checked the load in her pistols. "Not plannin' on it, but someone needs ta be watchin' ya back."

Hunter smiled grimly, "True enough."

The captain adjusted his grip nervously while he crawled up the dugout tunnel towards the surface. Just when he could see trees and sky, he adjusted the grip on his pistol, then eased up to look above the surface of the snow. A few feet from him stood William with his back against a tree. Angela, still in her werewolf form, crouched within reach of William with her teeth bared at two large, upright, white-furred beasts.

Neither creature seemed eager to attack, but both seemed tense. Perhaps it was William and Angela's appearance from under the snow, or simply uncertainty on how to deal with the snarling were-girl. As quietly as he could, Hunter pulled himself out of the hole and onto the loose snow. He paused to get his balance, and snow crunched lightly against his weight. Neither of the beasts moved, their attention still focused on the pair at the base of the tree. The captain sidestepped carefully away from the hole and raised his pistol, but the moment it was even with the creatures, the snow erupted around him in a storm of white.

"Bloody hell!"

A quick step backwards avoided the reach of two more creatures that were to either side of him. Captain Hunter spun towards the one to his right, whipping the barrel of his pistol across the side of the creature's face. It howled and fell backwards into the snow. Without pause, Hunter turned to the one on his left, only to face a bow with a drawn arrow. Light glinted off the metal arrowhead pointed at his chest. The captain's gaze followed the arrow back to its owner. At the other end of the bow, beneath the snow-dusted, thick fur was a weathered, tanned, human face with a white wrap over the mouth. As the wind stirred the branches overhead, causing a light puff of snow to drift downward, neither Hunter or the furred man opposite moved. Off to his left, four more of the men in furs emerged from the forest, bows at the ready.

Finally, the bowman nodded at Hunter's weapon and slowly relaxed the hold on his bowstring. Unsure, Hunter waited, which elicited a few harsh words from the bowman's guttural language. Again, the furred bowman nodded at Hunter's weapon, then relaxed the tension on his bowstring. Outnumbered, Hunter did the only thing he thought would spare lives. He lowered his own pistol slowly with a heavy sigh of frustration.

"Cap'n?" William called out from a few feet away.

"Stand down, Will. I don't think they mean us harm." Angela snarled at the pair in front of her. "I don't like their smell." Hunter slowly dropped his pistol into its holster. "I daresay they are not fond of yours, young lady. Withdraw the claws and stand easy."

Angela eased off her posture, but did not transform back to her human form. William likewise let go of some tree branch he had been using as a club.

"Aye, Cap'n. Just sure hope ya know what yer about."

"I do also, William. Though I daresay we have little choice."

It was young Miles and youthful innocence that finally bridged the gap between the groups. So accustomed to helping with O'Fallon's wounds, once free of the cave Miles automatically grabbed a small medical bag from William, then offered bandages and antiseptic to the tribesman Hunter had struck across the face. Without a complaint, Miles helped dress the cuts and offered an endless stream of questions and comments. Some of these the tribesman seemed to understand, others he did not. Nonetheless, the tribesmen's attitude did soften. It was as though if Miles' attitude removed some unknown suspicion in their minds.

Slowly, an uneasy alliance formed between the small group of airship sailors and the mountain tribe-folk while the snow was cleared away to recover what of the sailors supplies survived the avalanche. After recovering what they could, the long hike down-slope through the snow began. The first hour, the group moved in silence until they stopped under a rocky outcrop for shelter against the sharp mountain winds.

Hunter blew on his hands and rubbed them together against the cold. He glanced at Angela who, still in her part-wolf form, turned her gaze towards the snow at her feet.

"Young miss? I believe you had an explanation?"

"Yes Sirrah." She took a deep breath and exhaled slowly. "I'm not Miles' sister proper. Though, that's kinda obvious now I guess." She hesitated, sighed and pushed onward. "My own mum, she was the housekeeper for Miles' parents. When they were off and away, she looked after Miles and myself."

"So where is your mother now?"

"She's passed on, Sirrah. Two summers back a fever took her. There wasn't anythin' the doctors could do. Mum took ill so very fast. There wasn't much they could be doing. Miles' parents took me in as their own. Even with my … problem." She shivered uncomfortably against the cold. "They said they wanted to adopt me. Before they did, they got asked to go off on some trip. We had to stay with Miles' father's brother."

"Uncle Ian," Miles chimed in.

"He was nice enough, I suppose." Angela exchanged a glance with Miles. "Not much raised a voice - only a few times, when we didn't follow the rules he set down at home. Didn't let us out much unless we were watched. We really didn't go too many places outside his home."

Moira joined them, offering a leather waterskin filled with a heady, dark broth. "The hunters there think we be needin' a good swig or two. It'll warm ya, I'll give you that."

"Ladies first." Hunter said and nodded towards Angela. The young girl managed a smile and took a small drink. Miles followed suit a moment later. Hunter took a drink himself, then handed the waterskin back to Moira with a thin smile.\

"Thank you Moira. Have the others had some?"

"Nay a drop yet, about to pour some down O'Fallon's rum gullet. Might do him a bit o' good." With a grin, she walked around and over to O'Fallon and William.

The captain returned his attention to the two children. "How long have your parents been away?"

"Just upwards to a year." Miles said with a touch of sadness in his voice. "But they said they'd send for us once it was safe."

Hunter frowned. "Your father and mother, they are scholars of a sort?"

Miles beamed with pride. "They're historians."

"Mother is a scientist, Father is a historian." Angela corrected her brother firmly.

"S'what I meant."

Captain Hunter interrupted quickly. "Your uncle, Ian, sent us to rescue you once news reached him in London that your airship was overdue. Is that where you two were going? To meet your parents?"

Angela nodded, "Yes Sirrah, Uncle said that Mother and Father were expecting us at the ruins of Northumbrage. He packed us straight away, and found the first airship heading there."

"Northumbrage?"

"Yes Sirrah."

"I see." The captain looked over to where O'Fallon was rising slowly to his feet under the close watch of William and the tribesmen. "Well my dear, somehow we'll return you to your parents. Although, you were the one sneaking about the camp were you not?"

Angela looked at the ground, a faint touch of pink showed faintly around her eyes while she blushed.

"I'll take that as a yes. Next time, mind yourself skulking about an encampment like that. You could've been grievously hurt. Am I clear?"

"Yes Captain."

"Good. Now, go see if you can help William with O'Fallon. I suspect our stoic hosts are becoming eager for us to quit this place." The children ran past Moira in William's direction. She watched them a moment, lifted and adjusted her backpack's weight on her shoulders, and joined Hunter while he lifted his own pack.

"S'what do you think?"

"About what, pray tell?"

She smirked. "About the story they're tellin'. Ya believe 'em?"

"As much as they think it's the truth, yes. Now is it the truth? Mind you dear, no, I think it's half-truths at best. I believe they know only what they know. There are loose threads to weave of their story. The most obvious is that the uncle stated they were bound for Port Camden, yet they believe Northumbrage. Neither are within five days sail from each other. Also, why did he send them alone? I would think a relation would accompany them back to their parents?"

"If he's na' good with children, the though of goin' with 'em may not have come ta him." Moira commented.

"Perhaps. I still feel like something is wrong here. It feels rather dire."

"Somethin' more to mix the fuel, then. Angela mentioned to me in passin' that their Uncle was quite steady in checkin' over their parents' home. Always had the children with him, askin' if they saw anythin' out o' place in every room. She said it was a regular weekly outin'."

"A slight obsessed fellow."

"Aye, true that."

Hunter looked over at two of their guards. "The concern of what to do about the children and their uncle comes later. Foremost are our stoic hosts. Have you been able to understand them? I've had little luck on my own."

"Nary a word. What they're speakin' sounds odd, na something I've heard. William's been tryin ta work it out. He's quick with languages. May have figured it, by now."

"When the chance happens, we need to ask."

A grunt and a firm tap on the shoulder alerted Hunter to the tribesman that had walked up, unheard, behind him. The captain stood and brushed the snow from his clothes. "Leaving so soon? Well lead on Sirrah, shan't be late eh?"

The tribesman's expression showed no emotion or reaction to the comment. He pointed down the thin, snow-covered trail that wound its way downslope, and said something in his guttural language.

"Right, then." Hunter sighed and walked over to take his turn pulling O'Fallon on a hastily-carved litter.

Chapter 10

A few miles above the mountains, the *Griffin* slipped through the stray mist of white clouds. Her gas bag was tight and the rear propellers turned slowly. Aboard, Tonks looked over the edge of the ladder to the forward cargo hold of the *Griffin*. Krumer walked among the short stacks of crates below deck, carrying a clipboard. The first mate would pause a moment, review the list on the clipboard then inspect the particular crate of interest for signs of damage.

"Mr Whitehorse?"

Krumer looked up from the crate that held his attention. "Eh?"

"Doc has something."

"Good!" Krumer crossed over and scaled the ladder, leaving the worn wooden clipboard to sway gently from a small loop of twine.

Tonks stepped back when Krumer appeared above. "Doc didn't say much but sent word he'd gotten something interesting out of that bug."

Krumer snorted and rolled his eyes at the comment before he walked towards the rear of the ship. "Spirits willing, Doc and his talent for understatement could rankle even a shaman."

Tonks fell into step alongside Krumer. "Must be good, though.

I heard tell he's got that 'look' about him."

"Look? What look?"

"Ya know the one. The 'I've got ya' look."

"Ah that one."

The pair descended below deck again into the rear cargo hold. However, instead of holding cargo, a room had been built into the back that served as an on board hospice. Krumer knocked on the partially open door.

"Enter." Replied a thin, almost nasal voice.

Krumer pushed the door open and slipped inside. Tonks followed after.

"Tonks tells me you have learned something, Thorias. You've taken the bug apart, then?"

The man within put down the pen he had been using to write notes in his logbook. Thorias Llewellyn, usually known as 'Doc' to most of the crew, was a tall, thin figure with long brown hair an deep blue eyes. Fastidious, even for an elf, his appearance was often neat and trim. His black vest was brushed, white shirts pressed - or as pressed as a shirt may be aboard a privateer airship - and his long chestnut, brown hair pulled back and tied neatly behind him. Even his cutlass of Toledo steel that hung on the wall looked as it had been polished that very day. He leaned back from the small desk and gave the first mate a sour look. The brass dragonfly bug buzzed it's wings, then let out a brief squeak at the idea of being taken apart.

"Mr. Whitehorse, I did no such thing. Nor will I. Clockworks, like this little bug here, are rare and considered a living being. I'd no more 'take him apart' than I would you, Sirrah. Unless it was to remove another bullet from your tough orcish hide."

"Birds are natural. That's a machine." Krumer snorted.

"He says his name's Arcady. He's also got feelings that you're stepping on as sure as if you'd kicked him." Thorias replied sharply.

"Arcady?"

"Yes. Automatic Rewinding Clockwork Dragonfly. ARCDY or 'Arcady'."

"You don't wind a bird."

Tonks tried to suppress a laugh at the argument and managed only to turn it into a cough. Quickly he interjected, "Well all right then, but ya did learn something?"

Doc Thorias raised an eyebrow at the pilot. "Of course I did. Wouldn't have sent word, otherwise. This little fella's a fountain of information. When no one's tryin' to threaten him, that is. Seems he was given out to a mercenary company. Some bunch called RiBeld. Heard tell of them?"

Krumer frowned in thought while Tonks sighed and nodded. "Aye, that I do. High priced mercenaries started by Archibald RiBeld. RiBeld was supposedly some duke. The fourth duke of Collinsway, some little place North of London. The whole company is ruthless to ever single man-jack of them."

Thorias nodded in agreement and glanced around. The small hospice served as the doctor's home as well as its intended purpose to treat the infirm. He often kept personal amenities stashed about the room. He reached back to a small table nearby and scooped up a tall bottle with an amber colored liquid in it. "Then that would agree with the rest of the story, now wouldn't it? Charybdian Brandy? No? Well, pardon me while I have a quick sip."

He retrieved a small tumbler from another hidden cabinet and poured a little of the brandy into the glass for himself. "Where was I? Oh, RiBeld. Our little friend here was around when RiBeld got their orders. They were sent out to chase down that merchant ship, the *Marie Celeste*, and bring it down before it reached Northumbrage. They came upon her right before dusk and caught the crew unaware. Seems they meant to board her then scuttle her, but RiBeld's men got a bit carried away with the grapeshot. Tore the *Celeste* from here to Iceland. The *Celeste* and her crew got wise quick enough though. They fired up some smoke pots to try and cover their tracks into a cloud bank over the mountains. That's when the mercenaries lost them."

Krumer folded his arms over his chest. "Though the *Celeste* didn't make it to port at Northumbrage, but instead dove into the snow while trying."

The doctor shrugged and sipped his brandy. "I s'ppose. Little fella didn't see that part. Though RiBeld and his men looked, apparently they lost their victim among the clouds. On reporting back, their employer hired some trackers ... merchant marines ... with some history of taking risky jobs and pulling through."

"Us," Tonks said flatly.

Thorias smiled thinly and raised his glass in a small toast to the answer. "Yes. Us. Now the little fella here was sent along quietly. Hidden among some supplies we took on. Arcady was to keep an eye on us and report back where we were going."

"And when we found the *Celeste*." Finished Krumer.

"Exactly."

Tonks scratched a shadow of whiskers on his cheek and spoke in a low aside to Thorias. "Doc, can this little bug understand all we say?"

"Oh, Arcady's a fair grasp of proper English. Doesn't use it when he's scared mind you." The doctor leaned forward a bit and whispered. "Bit of a stutter when he's rattled."

Tonks sighed and looked at the brass clockwork dragonfly. Arcady turned its ruby colored eyes up at the pilot then shifted its weight uneasily. The sound of tiny muffled gears whirred gently in the moment of silence of the room. Tonks cleared his throat, then pushed on with what he wanted to ask. "So, you know who hired RiBeld then?"

With a single nod, the clockwork insect turned to face a blank wall. A glimmer of light shone from within the ruby eyes. The light grew brighter, more intense until a series of moving pictures, colors muted and laced with a touch of static, appeared. At first the scene was of a damp cobblestone road, lined with the characteristic brownstone London buildings, and lit by lamps against an approaching evening. A pair of figures appeared down the lane, then walked to a nearby door and waited. Then the view changed, bobbing gently like a small cork upon water, or as if the person who carried the source of the recording walked forward. Closer, and closer still, the view altered until the pictures angled upwards towards three figures backlit by the gas lamp overhead. Their faces were obscured by the overhead light , however, Arcady had been able to get a long, clear look at what each figure wore and a few obvious personal possessions such as an exquisite pocket watch.

The first mate frowned. "Yet we can't see their faces. Though at least we've idea what they almost look like."

Arcady fluttered his wings. From a hidden speaker a small voice - tinged with an artificial, stiff accent that emphasized the sound of the letter 't' just a little too much - spoke, "It was all I could see. I was in a pocket. It was not much."

Tonks had leaned forward, trying not to be distracted by how Arcady could actually display these images, with a look of concentration on his face. "A might more than that's there, I'd say. That suit and velvet vest, I remember such tailoring from the more finer shops in London. It's expensive and only the more well ta do bought such. Wait, can ya go back a bit ... if ya can do that with what your doin'?"

"Certainly."

The images halted then moved backwards for a few seconds while the dragonfly rewound the sequence. With a static burst and flicker, the pictures moved forward again.

The pilot pointed when a bronze pocket watch, etched in gold and silver came into view, then scrambled for a scrap piece of paper and a pencil. "Right there. If you look close you can see it. Hold it right there. I think I can sketch most of that out."

In moments they had a crude sketch of family coat of arms. There, among a field of ivy, was a modest shield with blood drops on which there was a black lion decorated with gold drops. Above that was a blue bar or 'chief' which held three silver scallops.

Thorias leaned forward, "But whose is it?"

Tonks raised his eyebrows in surprise when recognition came to him. "I only know a' one coat of arms like that. That belongs to the Patterson family."

Krumer looked up in surprise. "As in Ian Von Patterson? Our employer?"

"The one and same."

"Why would he even consider such a thing? Especially being a well - respected industrialist and a gentleman. At least according to the papers."

Thorias cleared his throat. "More of interest to me is how indeed would he know the route the *Celeste* would take? Those flight paths are kept under lock and key. Strict security you know."

"Nary a clue. But I can think of those that may know." Tonks said with a growing smile. "RiBeld and his men."

"Preposterous!" Thorias exclaimed. "You'd not get them to talk and besides, you'd have to find one alone."

"Alone I'm still planning about. However the where shouldn't be that hard. They're following us, so we just need to scout around for signs of them and see them before they see us."

The small tin voice emerged from the clockwork dragonfly. "Would this be useful sirs?" With a brief click, another series of pictures displayed on the wall. This time it was navigational charts marked with various routes and timetables. Some of which included today.

Before anyone could speak, the dragonfly shifted his weight

and did a close approximation of a rather human-like shrug. "When they were not throwing knives at me, they left me alone in the captain's cabin. I grew bored."

Chapter 11

An hour later, a steambat biplane sat on a level clearing far upslope from where the avalanche came to rest. The plane was largely in good working order, save for a set of bullet holes torn through the thin layer of rhino hide and canvas that composed the 'skin' of the craft's body. Steam jetted in hot geyser-like spouts through the holes in response to the rise and fall of the pressure from the aircraft's boiler.

Hard at work with a spanner wrench, a man in black cotton trousers, leather boots and a worn leather coat leaned into an open side panel that exposed the steam engine to the air. The man tugged furiously at the spanner wrench to tighten, or attempt to tighten, one of the pipe fittings collars that had been flush against the engine itself. Recently the pipe fitting had been doing its job well, until it had been struck by a bullet and belt oddly out of shape. Another sharp tug and the fitting moved just a fraction of an inch before the pipe itself ruptured. Steam exploded out of the engine compartment, knocking the pilot across the snow. He landed with a dull thump in the snowdrift, then groaned in pain. Slowly he reached under his coat to clutch at a bloody bandage-covered bullet wound in his shoulder.

Fifteen feet behind the wounded pilot, Tonks peered over the edge of some rocks until only the top of his head could be seen. He watched while the wounded pilot struggled painfully to his feet to slowly walk back towards the steam biplane. Quietly, Tonks slipped over the top of the rocks and walked silently across the snow. Just out of arm's reach, he cleared his throat with a smirk.

"Afternoon, Sirrah."

The pilot spun, a clockwork-needler pistol in hand. He was surprised to find himself staring into the barrel of Tonks' own revolver.

"Ah now, none a' that." Tonks said reproachfully.

"Who're ya, eh?" The man demanded in a mild Irish accent.

"The one who your goin' to be tellin' about why you're here, what all you're up to, and why the *Marie Celeste* is so all important to Archie RiBeld."

"Get bent!" He replied and raised his needler for a better aim.

"I wouldn't if I were you. I might miss. You probably won't with that needle-slinger of yours. But once you've done me in, what'll you do about the rest?"

"Rest a' who?"

A rough voice, touched with a hint of amusement, was heard from the other side of the steambat biplane. "Us."

Krumer walked into view, long barreled Colt pistol in one hand and cutlass in the other. He was dressed as he usually was - short boots, trousers and shirt - but over that he had wrapped himself in a white leather, fur trimmed cloak. On either side of him six more of the *Brass Griffin*'s crew, dressed in similar fashion to Krumer, rose from the snow itself near the edge of the clearing.

"Dahm' yer eyes, ya stinkin' glocky mutcher!" The man swore while he relaxed the grip on his weapon.

"Such language. An here I thought I was bein' hospitable. Well, maybe you'll learn a bit o' manners once we have ourselves a chat, eh?" Tonks stepped forward and took the pistol from the man.

Tonks nudged the wounded pilot towards the east, away from the clearing and towards where the *Griffin*'s longskiff lay hidden beyond the trees. Behind them, Krumer and two of the *Griffin*'s crew set to work pulling the blocks from the biplane to move it under cover nearby.

A short ride on the longskiff took Tonks, the Irishman and the rest of the landing crew back to the *Griffin*. Behind them, the steambat was neatly concealed beneath the thickest section of trees along the edge of the clearing. Once aboard, they secured the wounded pilot in a storage closet located in the forward hold - used most often to securely transport coal or other minerals. Despite his arguments to treat the man in his own hospice, Thorias nonetheless took his usual care in tending the Irishman's shoulder wound.

Two hours later, Thorias scaled the ladder from below. On deck he took a deep breath and adjusted his shoulder bag of medical supplies. Arcady flew up into view then circled the doctor in a lazy spin. Over near the main mast, Tonks noticed the pair and nodded a silent greeting. Thorias and Arcady walked over to Tonks while the pilot finished coiling some of the extra lengths of rope for rigging.

"How's Irish doing, Doc? His shoulder wound was bleedin' pretty good on the trip back."

"Natural to expect it, when one doesn't rest from a bullet

wound. Though his own ministrations to his wound had been adequate enough, now he'll mend with only a slight scar now instead of a rather ugly one."

"And so you tossed his chances at a good tale or two at a pub." Tonks laughed and tied off the end of the rope to a nearby belaying pin.

"I'm confident he'll embellish. I do wish I had been allowed to work on him in my own hospice instead of an old coal bin of a closet."

"It's more secure there and you know it."

"Perhaps, I doubt though he'd cause mischief. We're miles off ground. Anything he did would put himself in peril." Thorias rubbed his eyes as bright sunlight broke the thick clouds for a moment.

"Can't disagree with you there. Desperate men do strange things, if he's of a mind to. We found a few things aboard his steambat - a medical satchel with a pair o' logbooks, a compass and a few rolls of bandages stood out the most."

Thorias frowned. "I don't follow you. Why are those important?"

Tonks leaned backwards slightly to stretch his back a moment. "The satchel not so much. I'm thinkin' he grabbed it for the bandages. What he didn't count on was them logbooks. Top one was empty. Second had just started to be used by the captain of the *Celeste*. The satchel had been burnt all along one side. I'm no expert mind you, but I know a good burn from a lightning cannon when I see it. Irish down there had been ta the wreck. After our own had visited it I'll wager. Which means he's got to be one of RiBeld's men."

"Hard to find flaw there, Sirrah. Arcady, did you ever see him among RiBeld's rabble?"

Arcady settled on Thorias' shoulder and nodded. "Yes. I know him from my time aboard. He never saw me but I remember him."

Tonks folded his arms over his chest. "Did he say anythin' about the Captain and others that went a'ground with him?"

The clockwork insect sighed - a rather distinctive sound much like a very tiny bellows - shook his head slowly. "No, he did not speak of any such information."

"Then mayhap he'll need convincing. I'll try my hand at it." Tonks walked toward the ladder and descended below decks.

"I just finished putting him together, Tonks, I'd appreciate it if you not ruin my work!" Thorias called after the pilot.

Below deck and in the forward hold, Tonks drew an iron key from a vest pocket and turned it in the large steel padlock on the door latch. The lock clicked apart and the pilot eased the door open. To call the room a closet was a slight disservice to the room itself. It was small, but not tiny. It was a full five feet wide and fifteen foot deep - the wooden walls permanently stained with black soot marks and deep cuts. Long planks normally lined the walls as shelves but most had been removed save for one that could serve as a bench and sleeping pallet. Normally used for coal or other similar storage, the small room was now occupied by a surly Irish pilot.

"Well, if it nae be the talk'tive one. Come tae show me ya hospitality? Be teachin' me ma manners?"

"Any more'n I'll leave ya here ta enjoy the coal dust! If yer quite through, I've a question or two for you."

The Irishman laughed. "Ye be roit daft! Bein' shot down, den trussed up here like a winsome goose fer mid-Winter feast nae be makin' my own disposition kindly tae ye. Nae know of a reason Ah'd want tae answer anything ye be askin."

"Look Irish, we know your workin' with RiBeld on some skulduggery. The way I see it, you could be comin' out better than the rest o' your band about now."

"Get bent!" The Irishman barked another rude laugh at Tonks.

The pilot sighed, his patience frayed. "Gonna be that way is it? We can sail to that port." Tonks took a slow breath, then leveled a hard stare at the Irishman. "We found that satchel you pinched from the wreck. You should'a checked the second book. The captain of the *Celeste* had just started ta use it. That means you been there."

Sitting in a moment of stony silence, the Irishman glared at Tonks. Color flushed the prisoner's face. "Ya cannae be provin' a thing! I claim salvage rights!"

Tonks own temper rose to match the Irishman's. "We've people down in all that snow and trees, eh? A word from you where they went would be turnin' the tide in the right direction for everyone! RiBeld and his damn butchers wouldn't know, we'd send you off on whatever port you wish."

"Help ye? Ye own people shot me!" The Irishman spat on the deck at Tonks' feet.

Enraged, Tonks grabbed the man by the front of his dirty linen shirt and hauled him to his feet and slammed him against the wall. "So you were there! Talk ta me you snake! Or so help me I'll throw you overboard myself!"

"Ye don't have the stones!"

"Oh?" The pilot jerked the man so hard that he ripped the Irishman's shirt and accidentally bounced the mercenary off the doorframe. Slipping from the larger man's grasp, the Irishman fell to the floor then scrambled to stay out of Tonks' reach. Unfortunately for the Irishman, the room was only so large and Tonks latched on again like a tiger might grab its prey before dragging him from the room.

"Stop! A'ight! Stop!"

Tonks glared at the man with a white hot anger. "Talk then!"

"RiBeld's havin' us play the devil agin' some bunch dat t'were prowlin' around the wreck. 'None be leavin' the mountain', says he. 'Why', asks some o' us. 'Cause dat be what our pay's for', says he. He be tellin' us dat there tae be no survivors. So we try shootin' 'em. Wily buggers ye people are, they slipped away on us then. So's me wingman get's himself an idea. See, we'll start an avalanche. We pinched enough watches and such from the wreck tae prove there be no survivors he says. I ha' been shot so's I set down while he's off droppin' the bloody mountain on any down there. Cept' they found some cave. Made their way loose and headin' around towards the Yeti. Cannae be more'n hours ahead now. They'll be on foot if the Yeti hav'nae taken 'em!"

"Yeti? No such thing! Talk straight!"

"Ah be! Ah be! Ah be seein' 'em with me own eyes! Thick furred and strong they be wit' some sorta long claws. Likely be tearin' a man's head from his shoulders!"

Tonks hauled the man back to the closet and pushed him in.

The Irishman collapsed in a heap against the wooden bench. "Nae be tellin' RiBeld will ye? Ye dinnae know what he'll be doin' tae those dat talk. Flog the skin from me back he would! Lashes at the rail, or even the yard arm!"

His hand on the door, Tonks anger cooled somewhat. In his past he had worked for a mercenary company or two and had seen both good and bad. What little he had heard of RiBeld tended toward the latter. "You coulda been more cooperative, but it's the captain's call once he's back." Tonks hesitated and his softer side won out. "I'll pass a good word along ... if what you say plays true."

The padlock snapped shut with a hollow echo in the dark cargo hold. Tonks turned and dropped the key into his pocket to return to the keybox upstairs just outside O'Fallon's quarters. He quickly turned on his heel and stalked towards the ladder. Yeti? Avalanche? Tonks shook his head and shuddered involuntarily.

"I gotta a bad feelin' about this."

Chapter 12

The slow warmth of the fire pit spread through the one story room. Tendrils of smoke wound its way along thick, dark wooden beams that braced the gently arched rooftop and out small, concealed holes. Smoke drifted lazily through the holes but not the warmth. Rich, dark stone formed the foundation of the room and supported the wooden walls that began where the stone stopped a few feet off the floor. Rough woven linen and furs had been laid out around the long room to surround the fire pit. Empty hooks and pegs - normally used for weapons - adorned two of the walls in between narrow shuttered windows. The back wall was covered by a rough linen tapestry alive with a multicolored array of mosaic patterns in an abstract shape of a gigantic eagle in flight. Hunter paced the length of the stone long house like a caged wolf. His coat had long since been tossed aside onto the furs, leaving the captain to pace and storm about in his rolled-up shirtsleeves, vest, trousers and dark leather boots.

Moira looked up from her place by the fire where she sat examining the broken pieces of the opti-telegraphic. "Pacin' the room will nae solve much. Ye'll be stewin' up into a temper."

Hunter scowled toward the wooden door at the front of the long house. "A margin of length too late for that."

"O'Fallon?"

"Indeed. We've been in their village for at least two hours, most of that they've been treating him."

"Ah'm sure they're doin' what they can. William said they be havin' somethin' about treatin' strangers with respect."

William shrugged from where he sat on the far side of the fire near Angela and Miles. "It 'twas what they said." The young man paused, then blushed a little and mumbled. "Least wise it sounded like it."

Moira smiled at William to reassure him. "Ah nae think ye be wrong about it. Ah spied more'n one bullet wound on a few a' their own. Look ta be treated well enough and they were walkin' about. Ah'd also be thinkin' that if they wanted ta do us ill, they'd leave us out in the snow."

Hunter sighed and turned away from the door that had not opened on its own despite his worst scowl. "Point well taken. So, found any inspiration with the opti-telegraphic?"

"The bullet tore the casing open near the key lock itself. Outside a' that, we be havin' two gears bent, one locknut's missin' and a secondary windin' spring got itself caught on one o' the bent gears and stretched outta shape. I'm more'n a little surprised it didn't break. Quite a mess really."

"Do what you can with it. If the contraption has at least some life left, try and get a message out. Something the Griffin could track on to find their way here."

Moira nodded briefly. "Very well Cap'n. Right away."

Angela looked up from the fire. "Cap'n? Sirrah?"

"Yes, Angela?"

"Will the pirates find us?"

Hunter hesitated a moment. "I don't know for certain my dear, but I hope not. They should believe we were buried by their avalanche. Provided they don't go to ground and check beneath the trees, they won't find what really happened to us."

"But what if they do?"

"We'll deal with that when it comes then. No worries now."

Behind them, at the front of the room, the door opened with a slight creak of protest. Through the doorway stepped a Yeti warrior. He was shed of the coat of mottled white fur from before. Instead, he wore thick linen tunics, trousers and a brightly-colored woolen vest. He still bore the angry red bruise where Captain Hunter had punched the tribesman across the face in the fight on the mountainside. The Yeti warrior gestured towards Hunter with his bow and then pointed out the doorway.

"I take it we are to go with you? In that case, I'll want one of my crew along." Hunter replied and pointed towards William Falke, then himself, then to the doorway. The Yeti looked at both men and nodded once then stepped back from the doorway then looked expectantly towards the two men.

William grabbed his woolen coat and slipped it on quickly. "I think he's wanting us to go first."

Captain Hunter scooped up his own coat and slipped it on in anticipation of the chill outside. "I suspect you are correct William.

We'd best oblige."

Outside the door, William and Hunter were met by a second and third Yeti warrior. The two guards looked the two airship sailors over once then turned to walk away. A firm push from the Yeti warrior behind them encouraged Hunter and William to step lively to catch up.

The path the Yeti guards took led them to another stone and wooden building much like all the others in the village. The difference in this one was that it was much older and longer with its rear stone walls flush up against the foot of a rocky rise.

The front two guards stepped to either side of the main door. The Yeti that trailed behind stepped around Hunter and William. Without so much as a look, the warrior opened the door and slipped inside the building.

William fidgeted nervously. "Place has an important look to it."

Hunter's eyes were not focused on the building, but on the rise of rocks that both supported the village and gave it a natural commanding view of the area. The only place the Yeti were blinded to any view was where a natural rock shelter arched just slightly over the north-eastern corner of the village. That north-eastern corner where the two men stood.

"Most likely a village elder or person of some importance." The captain nodded, mostly in reaction to his own thoughts. "They are quite well-defended here. That overhang covers a large portion of this part of their village. See the scoring on the rocks there?"

"Aye."

"Lightning drake if I ever saw it. But this wouldn't help against fast-moving pilots with a few hand bombs to toss down. If I had to guess, the pirates push the locals back up in here, then come in force on the ground when the Yeti have lost the high ground advantage. Penned in, they cannot mount much defense as their natural defense is used to contain them."

William whistled low while the scene the captain described played out in his mind. "I see what ya sayin' Cap'n. It'd be over a'fore anything really started."

At that moment, the Yeti warrior opened the door wide, gestured to William and Hunter then pointed to inside the building.

Hunter glanced at William. "I do believe we have been summoned."

"Aye, Cap'n."

Beyond the door, the room was not much different than the one than the one which sheltered the *Brass Griffin*'s crew. Tight, fitted stones rose from the floor to meet dark, stained wood three feet off the ground. Above the ceiling was the same interlocked collection of smooth cut wood, except here there were small multi-colored cuts of linen. Each bit of cloth was no larger than four inches square, hung from the rafters. Furs and a few hide-covered stools were settled around the room. Most notably were the three older men seated near the large fire pit in the middle of the room. They were dressed modestly in long linen shirts, trousers and ankle high moccasins. Four Yeti warriors stood silently and alert at the corners.

The Yeti warrior that led Hunter and William spoke quietly with a tone of respect to the three older men. Not to say any of the three were feeble. Despite their obvious age, each still bore a well-muscled frame with a clear steady gaze. The oldest of the three nodded in reply to the young warrior whom nodded in return and retreated from the room.

A long moment of silence fell around the room while the three Yeti elders stared at Hunter and William. Unsure of what - if anything - to say, the pair returned the silence with some of their own. William shifted his weight and leaned over to Hunter after a moment.

"Chatty bunch ain't they Cap'n?"

"Indeed," was the captain's reply. However his mind was elsewhere. It was something about the decor or perhaps the demeanor of the three older gentlemen that reminded Hunter of a diplomat or admiral he knew from years ago. These were men of importance to the Yeti.

Finally the oldest of the three nodded once and gestured towards a set of furs on the far side of the fire.

"Iyotaka."

Hunter exchanged a look with William who shrugged. "Wants us ta sit, Cap'n ... I think."

"Quite."

Once seated on the furs, Captain Hunter cleared his throat. "Before anything else, I wish to offer my thanks for the assistance to my wounded man."

The three elders exchanged a look. William gave a nervous smile then - with the occasional stumbling and stuttering over unfamiliar words - provided a translation. One of the elders, the youngest of the three with only some gray shot through his coal dark hair, lifted a wooden cup of some hot, dark liquid and sipped at it before he replied.

"Toka sni. Takuwe niye lel?"

Immediately another of the elders looked shocked at his companions' question. He barked a fast, harsh reply. This set off a storm of conversation among the two younger of the three tribal leaders. The oldest sat calmly and drank his own drink as if nothing had happened.

Hunter tried his best to follow what he thought was an argument, but eventually gave up. "Will, what are they saying?"

William's eyes darted between the two arguing men, desperate to follow the rapid exchange. "Ah think the one asked us somethin' pretty blunt, but ah don' know the words. The other one there? He's got his boiler in a burn cause he's thinkin' the first was rude. Ah get the thought that they're supposed ta be polite ta strangers. Like what ah said before about them wantin' ta treat strangers with respect."

"Good for us then in a way, it confirms we won't be harmed soon. What about now?"

"They're just talkin' too fast for me Cap'n. Ah don' know some of those words ... Ah'm learnin' as fast as ah can suss 'em out."

Hunter was about to say something himself when the last elder spoke.

"Owajila."

Immediately the other two Yeti fell silent. Hunter himself had paused but quickly recovered.

"William, tell them if you would ..."

"Silence ... please."

Hunter stopped in mid-sentence at the graveled voice. The elder, who had been quiet through everything, spoke. He was careful with his words, as they were obviously not his native language, but words he had an acceptable command of, at least.

"The boy ... does not have to speak for you. I know some of your words."

William sat back in surprise. Hunter checked his own comment before he said it and instead cleared his throat.

"Well that puts a new spin on things. If I may, your grasp of them is quite good, Sirrah."

"Your people have come to here before. One stayed some time. A man of learning." The elder sipped his drink then set his cup down. "I am called Utawah."

"I am Anthony Hunter. This is one of my crew, William Falke."

William inclined his head in greeting. "Sirrah."

Utawah watched them both a moment before he replied. "Good meeting. I must be ... forward. My companions wish to know when will your people stop attacking?"

William's mouth fell open. "Tain't us! We been shot up and shot at and chased about like rabbits!"

Hunter waved William quiet. "Utawah, it has been none of my people that have harmed yours. Myself and my crew are recent visitors, Sirrah. We have no reason to cause injury."

The chieftain leaned forward, the light of the fire cast lurid shadows along his weathered face. "So say you. My people suffer many burns and cuts. Some have lost arms and fingers with your attacks. We just want it to stop. We will give you what we can, but know we will fight you."

Hunter shook his head. "Utawah, those vile creatures are not of my crew. My own country would have dealings with them if they knew what they were about. This I assure you." At the elder's unconvinced look, Hunter paused and took a different approach. "Very well, if we were one group and the same, why would we be here if we could simply attack you again as you say we already have?"

"This we do not know. That is why you and your followers have been brought here. We are curious as to why."

Sitting quietly next to Hunter, William had managed to restrain himself for as long as he could. "Because we tain't with 'em!"

"Will!"

"Cap'n, sorry for the disrespect, but they tain't payin' attention!" William returned his frantic look to Utawah. "If'n we were in with them pirates, why'd we drag one o' our own over the snow and ice when he's so bad hurt? Why'd them pirates in the steambats try and bury us in half the bloody mountain?"

Utawah smiled slightly, "I agree with what you say. It is my companions that are more ... suspicious. I will relay your words."

Hunter sat forward. "Utawah, if you would, please relay this. We are being hounded by the same men that hunt your people. They seek two children in our care for reasons I believe are quite dire. I fear for the children's safety more than I do ours. The longer we argue, the longer we wait, the closer they come to finding us again. This time, they will find your village, if they have not anticipated that we would find our way here already. We can help you."

Utawah paused. "If we return your weapons to you."

Hunter nodded. "Indeed and trust us with them. I understand that asks a great deal. If that is too much, then do what you will with us but hide the children. At least that... if nothing else."

Utawah stared unblinking at Hunter in silence. Then the elder chief turned to the other two and spoke rapidly in their own dialect.

Embarrassed, William leaned over to Hunter and whispered. "Cap'n I ..."

"Think nothing of it. I was caught in the moment myself."

"Think we convinced 'em?"

"I dearly hope so, William. For all our sakes."

William sat bolt upright as if stuck with a needle. "Cap'n ..."

Hunter's attention was riveted on the conversation across the fire from them. "Hm? What is it?"

"They're here!"

The explosion outside shattered the front door, the adjacent section of wall next to it and rained debris through the room.

Chapter 13

Hunter coughed then brushed at the cloud of dust that assailed his eyes. He staggered over broken stones and shards of wood, his mind clouded from the blast that had ripped the front of the building away. Blood teased the edge of his vision from a pair of cuts that traced grooves above his right eyebrow. Dirt smudged his clothes. Rough gravel peppered his hair. A light, cold wind tossed the torn remains of the colored cloth squares about him then lifted them up toward the heavens.

"William!"

There was no reply. Hunter tripped on a loose board and fell heavily into the dirt. With a grunt, he struggled to rise then felt a strong pair of hands grip his arm and help him to his feet.

"Good show, William."

"Not William," Utawah replied firmly.

The captain blinked, the grit finally free from his vision, and turned in surprise.

"Your man is there." Utawah pointed to where two of the Yeti slowly struggled with a heavy timber. Beneath it lay William, motionless with his eyes closed and limbs caught in a strange angle. A third waited to ease the young man from beneath the debris once it was safe to do so. It was plain to see that William had thrown himself at Utawah to knock the elder aside before the roof caved in on top of where the elder had been sitting. Hunter started to rush forward but Utawah stopped him.

"My people will tend him. Quickly, tell me, did you mean your words?"

Hunter scowled. Every instinct in him said to see to his crew, his responsibility. The captain's anger flashed hot and bright in his eyes when he shot a glare back at Utawah. "Quite!"

The chieftain pressed a sharpened bone dagger into the captain's hand. "Then do not squander the gift your man has given you."

A pause of a single heartbeat passed before the hint of a grin spread across Hunter's face. He grasped the knife firmly. "Indeed. Lead on then."

The two men raced from the ruined building to the chaos outside. Smoke poured out of holes in the roof numerous buildings. Other buildings were little more than burnt shells where the rooftops had collapsed in on themselves from the dynamite that had been dropped on them. Bodies lay strewn across the ground with smoke trailing from their backs. A lump caught in the captain's throat, he tried to swallow it down but he found he could not.

"Utawah... your people..."

Suddenly, a pair of steambats buzzed overhead like a pair of angry bees. High pressure jets of salt water guided arcs of electricity across the ground. Villagers screamed, either in pain or anger at the fliers above while they scrambled for whatever cover was nearby. Those that could not find any jerked and screamed when the electricity struck and threw them feet from where they had been.

Perhaps it was a light spray of water, or the crack of electricity. Without thinking, Hunter shoved Utawah to the right and then dove to the left. A scant second later, a bolt of lightning cracked against the broken timbers, then ground where the men had stood. Wood soaked from the salt water, then dried instantly with a blackened burn mark left behind. Electricity grounded itself all around in the nearest objects from rocks, stones and people. Two of the Yeti were thrown ten feet from where they stood. Utawah jerked from only a touch of the blast, Hunter was lifted into the air and slammed down against the stones in a fit of electrical induced convulsions.

Hunter sat up slowly. His entire body shook violently from suffering his portion of the electrical blast. Blackened skin and a line of reddish-veined burn streaks ran down his right arm where the sleeve had burned away from the attack. Pain shot through nerves and his head ached with the residual effect of the small, but powerful, jolt of lightning. The captain took a long, slow, ragged breath in an attempt to regain control over his own body. Utawah - who had fared slightly better as he had been knocked out of path of the attack - slowly got to his feet. The elder shook his head to clear the cobwebs from them before he looked over to Hunter.

"Are you well?"

His shakes subsiding, Hunter looked at the burnt and tattered glove that had covered his clockwork right hand. Bits of static still jumped between the fingers while he experimentally flexed it. Gears turned, miniature pistons flexed while his fingers moved a bit sluggishly. They had a willingness to adhere magnetically to each other. He took another slow experimental breath while his heart pounded hard in his chest, then winced while he looked at the unusual burn marks along his right arm.

"A few hard burns and a magnetized hand. Well, its not as if I fell from the back of a lightning drake at twenty feet off the ground." Convinced he and his hand were still none the worse for wear, he looked around, then up at the retreating steambat. "A dagger won't do. We'll need range."

Utawah offered a hand-up to the captain and shouted a command in his own language. Quickly a young Yeti warrior, perhaps no older than his late teens, raced off towards a smaller building that was no larger than perhaps a tool shed. Moments later the boy returned with a bundle. It was nearly as long as the young warrior, with bits of wood exposed at one end and wrapped entirely in a handwoven, woolen blanket. He dropped it on the ground and unwrapped it. Inside were several unstrung bows, quivers full of arrows and some leather bags beneath.

The elder chieftain knelt and lifted a bow and quiver of arrows. "This, if they are close enough. They have learned to stay away from our arrows ... mostly. Sometimes we find a way to reach them. That is rare now."

"Then we'll find a way to bring them closer."

Hunter had knelt to select his own bow when he saw a familiar tube of metal protruding from one of the small leather bags. Moving the bow aside, he opened the bag to find his gun belt and pistol inside. Alongside that lay Moira's pistols, O'Fallon's knives, and other weapons of the crew. Hunter freed his weapon and belt from the bag and automatically checked the pistol to see if it was still loaded. Another Yeti warrior approached. Hunter recognized the man from the bruise still visible on the man's face. It was the warrior he had fought in the woods. The captain tensed, however the Yeti merely looked at Hunter with a level, emotionless gaze and spoke a short comment in his own dialect. The captain looked to Utawah with a questioning look.

"He wishes you a good hunt." The elder smiled and fastened the quiver around his waist.

Hunter looked back to the Yeti warrior and strapped on his gun belt. "You as well, sir. Give them the proper hell." He turned back to the chieftain, "What of my crew? They'll need to defend themselves and could lend a hand chasing off these bloody blaggarts as well."

"It will be done." Utawah issued a rapid string of commands Hunter had no hope of following. The young Yeti nodded repeatedly, grabbed up the bundle and raced off for the building Moira and the rest were kept.

The warrior, the captain and the elder looked around. Smoke rose from burned buildings. Here and there, the braver members of the village stepped from the shelter of ruined homes. Some cried at the destruction, others stared in stony silence while the wounded were led towards the shelter of the natural rock overhang. Another few searched the bodies on the ground for friends and loved ones. Above all, the steambats were not to be seen.

Hunter shaded his eyes against the afternoon light. "Now,

where have the blighters gotten to?"

Abruptly, the two steambats broke into view overhead and began another strafing run at the village. Utawah, watching the angle of flight, turned to look at the arcing rock formation just behind them. He pointed and spoke to the warrior next to him. Immediately, the two men raced for the rocks and began to climb. Hunter did not understand what they said but understood the sentiment. Bows and arrows are not useful if the target remained out of range. One needed elevation to shorten the distance as best as possible. However, if the steambats pulled from their dive, the effort would be wasted.

The captain smiled while he finished his thought aloud. "Then the pirates need a reason not to change their attack."

Hunter planted his feet, out in the open and plain view. It was a fool's errand unless Hunter could distract the pilots and move fast enough to avoid the hungry tendrils of lightning. He drew his pistol with a deep breath and aimed. Twenty feet ahead of the captain, twin electrical bursts from the aircraft licked the ground, eating dirt in two blackened grooves. Hunter stood his ground, aimed and squeezed two shots, then raced for the safety of a ruined stone wall nearby.

The moment he reached the wall and threw himself over the side, the loud crackle of lightning stopped and the steambat banked overhead. Steam vented from holes in its side near the vehicle's boiler. In the cockpit, the pilot struggled with the controls despite the gout of steam that threatened to obscure his view. With a wild turn, the steambat broke off its attack, veered far right and climbed for the safety of the clouds and higher altitude. The very moment the steam-powered aircraft soared over the rocks, arrows rained down in a deadly shower.

More holes opened in the skin of the steambat that now turned and jerked even harder to escape.

Suddenly, a boom sounded once, then twice. Hunter jumped and spun to see Moira lower her pistols and swear violently as her bullets missed the second steambat. Despite its narrow escape, the second steambat flier banked left, then soared overhead without having fired at the village. The pilot shook his fist at Moira who snarled in return and spit in the man's direction. Arrows suddenly peppered the aircraft, driving the pilot to climb to a higher, safer, altitude away from village, bullets and arrows.

Hunter grinned and reloaded. "Good show. Overdue to give back what we've been suffering."

Utawah knelt on the rocks above them and grunted his disgust at the retreating flyers. "They stay away from our weapons and attack from far away. Today they've learned we can still touch them. Perhaps they leave us now."

Hunter slid his pistol into its holster and flexed his clockwork hand again, still suspicious it was damaged. Sparks of static continued to dance over the brass knuckles and exposed gears. "While I'd like to hope as much, I suspect otherwise. We dealt them a hard sting but nothing more. They'll return at some point."

"Cap'n!" Moira shouted and pointed at a shape above the tree line.

There, where the clouds were parted in a rough 'V' shape, a large airship slowly descended. It was long, easily twice as long as the *Griffin,* at possibly over one hundred and sixty feet or more. The vessel was held aloft by a large, tight gas bag and a trio of large propellers at its stern, or rear, of the ship. Hunter knew the configuration, as it was more commonly seen among military vessels. Two pair of steambats flew in escort around the larger ship like an airborne quartet of bodyguards. While they watched, one longskiff then another was launched from the massive airship. Both were loaded with personnel.

"Utawah, it seems we are about to receive some unwanted guests. We must be quick if we're to prepare a proper welcome."

Chapter 14

Clouds of inky black smoke hung low like a blanket over the village. Buildings, many ruined by explosions, stood at crazed angles in the gloom like broken, blackened teeth in a skull shattered under a boot heel. A thinner smoke coiled around walls and collected near windows and the ground. It formed a thin fog that veiled both alive and dead while it wound through the village and ran along the dirt paths into the forest. Within the fog, a strange, almost desperate stillness clung to the village like a dew on the ground.

Occasionally, the silence was pierced by a shout as one villager or another finally ventured out to locate a lost loved one. A mournful cry to a loved one that often lay among the fallen, or a shriek of despair at finding someone where they lay.

From downslope, closer to the thick stand of trees, two modest groups of armed figures approached. There were ten in each group, but both followed behind one lone man. Tall and thin with modest shoulders, the leader wore a long wool coat that brushed the tops of his ankles. Beneath was a well-kept - if not rather expensive - linen shirt, trim black vest, and dark trousers tucked into well-oiled leather boots. He walked with purpose, but also with a distinct air of raw arrogance. No closer than twenty paces from the edge of the village, he stopped to coolly glance down at the remains of a bird unfortunate enough to be caught in the initial village onslaught. He tapped it disdainfully with a boot.

"I send you people to recover two children," Archibald RiBeld said in a slightly clipped, harsh British accent, "herd a band of savages into submission so they are no trouble, and to capture - if not silence - one privateer captain and his misfit crew." He shoved the body of the bird onto its side with the toe of his boot. "Instead you give me ... this. Tell me, what do I pay you people for?"

One of the sailors from the first group, a younger man, looked at RiBeld and spoke up as he nervously fidgeted with his rifle. "Guv' ..."

An older, balding man with a scarred face hit the young man across the mouth with the back of his hand. "Das ist 'Captain' to yo'!"

The younger sailor recovered slowly from the blow. "m'sorry Mister Johanssen." He looked back to RiBeld. "Beggin' the Cap'n's pardon, but we's ha' na much choice. They'd surprised us on the mountainside."

RiBeld turned and leveled a gray-eyed gaze as cold as death on the younger man. "Ah, yes, so I understand." He smiled thinly which caused a wave of involuntary shivers in the sailor. The younger sailor wanted to look away but could not, any more than a rabbit would stare in horror at a hawk. "You were surprised. By two children, and four privateers! One of whom was mortally wounded!" The mercenary leader paused to take a breath and regain his composure. "Certainly ... after that news, we were all surprised." RiBeld turned his head toward the rest of the guard but kept his unblinking gaze on the younger man.

"Mister Johanssen!"

The balding, scarred sailor tugged his gray peacoat around him a bit more against the cold and stepped closer. "Ja, meine Captain?"

"Take the men and start from two ends of this rat's nest. Send them in towards that clearing near the middle and shake out any vermin that still cling to their hovels. Kill anything that moves."

"Ja. Und the kinder, Captain?"

"Bring the children to me ... alive. Von Patterson has been so very interested in making these children vanish as a means to control their parents. However, these children have cost me dearly. I'm inclined to see just how much more Von Patterson will pay for them so that he may continue his little family subterfuge."

"Ja, Captain."

"Good man." RiBeld hesitated a moment, then smiled just a bit wider, if not colder at the younger man who he still held frozen in front of him. "Johnny Tullins isn't it?"

"Aye," came the weak reply.

Archibald released the young man from his icy gaze and looked over to his first mate. "Johanssen? Take special care with our young, talkative friend here. Someone with such initiative to speak up should be ... molded."

The older man passed a brief look of sympathy to the younger man then nodded to RiBeld. "Ja ... Captain." The young sailor wilted slightly from fear.

Archibald kicked the body of the dead bird aside and walked toward the village. "Good man."

Fog played along the ground and around the feet of the men as they split up, then slowly entered the village from opposing sides. The few villagers that saw the group quickly disappeared into the ruins, using the heavy mist as cover for their retreat. Some of RiBeld's mercenaries sought to give chase, but the Yeti - having a better knowledge of the area - easily slipped out of sight.

At the village center, RiBeld kicked over the body of a dead Yeti warrior, burnt to death from the initial raid. He frowned at the corpse then frowned at the broken walls surrounding him.

Two of his own men joined him. In the distance, muffled shouts, punctuated by the occasional gunshot and shriek of pain, indicated where the rest of his mercenaries were. He mentally took note of the sounds, but gave them no further thought.

"Where ... are ... they?" He said slowly, pronouncing each word firmly in turn.

The soft metallic click of a gun being cocked close behind him - that surprised him. Carefully, RiBeld kept his hands still and slowly turned. His two bodyguards had already spun around with their backpack-powered lightning rifles brought to aim. Captain Hunter smiled pleasantly at the mercenary as if he were greeting an old friend for tea. Only this was not a friend he pointed his gun at. He took a step closer. Smoke curled along his coat and danced at his feet. The occasional pop of static raced along his brass fingers that gleamed in the dying light of the day.

Around the captain, Yeti warriors emerged from where they lay hidden behind ruined walls, beneath seemingly scattered blankets and other debris around the clearing. They moved as shadows and without any sound, like angry wraiths drawn to the source of their hatred with bows and arrows drawn.

"I'd say 'right here', though the statement would be redundant at this point."

RiBeld forced a thin smile. "Quite. The infamous privateer captain - Hunter isn't it?"

Hunter inclined his head a moment in agreement, "The same. You, Sirrah would be would be Archibald RiBeld?"

"You appear to have the advantage."

"As if I wouldn't take it, since you invited so many friends."

RiBeld forced that thin smile again. "I dislike small talk. So, shall we dispense with the pleasantries? What are your terms?"

Hunter adjusted his grip slightly, still worried his clockwork hand would stop functioning at any moment. "Right to the point. Indeed, I like that. My terms? You and your men to leave the area. Leave myself and my crew to our ship, and we go our separate ways."

"I'll not assume you are stupid."

"That would be wise." Hunter interrupted.

RiBeld scowled. "What of my contract with Von Patterson? I've made an agreement."

"Break it. This is a large, empty space on the Continent, Sirrah. Say we were lost among the snow, or at least lost from you. It wouldn't damage your reputation any, and I doubt it would be the first time you've lied on a contract."

That time, RiBeld's thin, bemused smile was not forced.

"Indeed. What of the children?"

"They leave with us, naturally."

"Ah, I'm afraid that is out of the question. They are specifically what our contract is over. You? Your crew? You're all incidentals and expendable. Perhaps a mild amusement for my men at best. No offense, mind you."

Hunter's jaw clenched at the comment. "None taken, though the children are not leaving with you. May I ask why they are so important?"

RiBeld chuckled nastily and shifted his weight. From behind the group of Yeti, RiBeld watched as a small knot of figures approached, then pause in the fog. After a moment, they slowly eased forward with weapons drawn. The mercenary captain cleared his throat and raised an eyebrow at Hunter. "You don't know, then? Well I suppose Von Patterson wouldn't have told you. They are a key, nothing more. Through them, he gains control over the children's parents. I doubt he minds much if the two cherubs are even delivered alive. Which is all the same to me. Dead weight is dead weight, as they say."

The captain choked on the rage that slowly built like bile in the back of his throat. Hunter had a strong dislike for snakes, even the kind that walked on two legs. He took a deep breath and bit back a string of harsh comments. Instead he choked out, "Why?"

"Why? Well, Von Patterson was rather reluctant over those details. Not that I mind, so long as I and my men are paid. I would assume some position of power, money, or perhaps both. As I said, that is not my problem, or yours, actually."

"Oh? And why isn't it mine? I daresay I think it is."

RiBeld's smile turned into a cold sneer. A malicious, cold gleam shone in the man's eyes. "You have far greater worries, my dear captain."

"Hunter!" The shout broke the tension in the air - and the conversation - like a rock shattering glass. Moira, suspicious over not hearing any message from Hunter within the past few minutes, had carefully stalked a winding path through the empty buildings. She was concerned he had done something rash or foolish and therefore was in trouble.

At her shout the knot of RiBeld's men - who had remained outside the clearing and behind the Yeti warriors - shouted in turn, a wordless cry of rage and battle lust. They released a deadly volley of gunfire at the Yeti warriors who had been around RiBeld, Hunter and the two guards. Warriors jerked and fell into the dirt. Some screamed at bloodly wounds, others lay motionless bleeding quickly out. The remaining Yeti released their arrows into the small group of RiBeld and his guards, the dove aside just before bullets tore the air and stone around them.

RiBeld dodged, then stepped behind his guards who took the brunt of the attack. One guard jerked wildly when arrows peppered his chest. The second fared slightly better as he fired a stream of high pressure salt water charged with electricity at Hunter before attempting to dodge the arrows that had missed his companion. Slowed by the backpack of salt water, he avoided any lethal arrows to his chest, but instead suffered them into his left arm and leg. Both from the shock of the wounds and unwieldy backpack, the man fell to the ground with a hard impact. His rifle fell from his grip into the dirt.

More arrows flew from Yeti hidden throughout the village. Several mercenaries, caught unaware, fell quickly before the rest scrambled into cover and returned fire with a deadly hail of bullets.

Lightning crackled along its stray jet of salt water and landed where Hunter had been. He had sidestepped just before the jet of water reached him, moving through the smoke that wound and danced between him and the guards. When the arrow felled the second guard, salt water sprayed into the air and created a shower that crackled with stray electricity sparking angrily in the air.

Hunter backed away, unable to see anything but the brief curtain of water in front of him. Once the shower dissipated, he saw RiBeld on the other side. In a blur of motion, the mercenary's hand flew to his gun, drew it and brought it to bear on Hunter faster than the eye could follow. Hunter's eyes went wide as he moved again, raising his own pistol at RiBeld. Smoke blossomed as they fired at point blank range.

Chapter 15

Hunter winced as one burning, white-hot sensation lanced through his right shoulder and another lower down through his side. Pushing past the pain he fired his pistol again, stumbling for the cover of a tumbled, smoke-covered rocks that lay only ten feet from him. Ten feet or one hundred, each step seemed to take longer the closer he got. At five feet, Hunter dropped to one knee, his gun smoking and exhausted.

Across from him, RiBeld was doubled over from his own pain. A bullet had torn through his thigh and another had burned a furrow along his arm, knocking the gun from his hand. He watched Hunter fall to his knees in a struggle to reach the only obvious cover. The mercenary captain grimaced at his wounds and drew a long knife from under his coat. In a half-run, half-limp, he charged towards Hunter, knife aimed for his spine.

Hunter turned to see the knife before it fell, alerted by some sound he could not place among the chaos. With a cry of surprise he caught RiBeld's wrist with his artificial left hand and hammered a hard right uppercut into RiBeld's midsection. Momentarily robbed of air, the mercenary wheezed roughly and slammed his own fist across Hunter's mouth. Unsteady already, both men fell into a brawling heap.

It was Hunter who gained leverage first, and shoved RiBeld to one side out of arm's reach. He looked around. Both Yeti and mercenaries were among the living and the dead that lay scattered across the village. Worry gripped him like a vice. He searched for any of his crew, Angela or Miles. Moira was only ten yards away behind cover and steadily firing at any mercenary unlucky or foolish enough to venture into the open. Of the children he saw no sign, until he heard Angela's shrill shout of panic. She raced across the clearing to the other side, then down a dirt path. Clothes torn, yelling the entire way, she looked like a diminutive banshee on the battlefield. Try as he might, Hunter could not make out what she said.

He looked in the direction she ran. Across the clearing and well back among the buildings, three Yeti warriors were in a prolonged knife fight with three mercenaries. The extended battle blazed in front of the door. Blades spun and glinted off the fading light while the men sliced and grappled close. So intent on the first three, the Yeti completely missed a fourth soldier that slipped past and raced for the door. He shoved it open and dashed inside.

Moments later, he careened back out of the doorway and into the dirt. A stool followed a moment later, smashing into the sailor with a solid impact. Behind that limped a pale, bandaged, bloodied and enraged Conrad O'Fallon, quartermaster of the *Brass Griffin*, brandishing another heavy wooden stool like an over-sized bludgeon.

The sailor snarled and got to his feet with a murderous look at O'Fallon. The badly wounded quartermaster spit at the mercenary then limped forward. He swung his stool but his wounds betrayed him as he missed. He fell hard from two sound punches on his bullet wounds that immediately started to bleed. The sailor then grabbed a broken shard of wood as long as a man's arm, and walked over. He stood over the quartermaster, a nasty sneer on his face, and raised the shard of wood for a killing blow.

Before he could stake O'Fallon into the ground, an ear-splitting roar made the sailor look up. The next moment, a brownish-black wiry, snarling mass of fur, teeth and claws shaped remarkably like Angela Von Patterson slammed the villain from his feet. He fell hard into the dirt, his makeshift weapon skittering across the dirt far beyond his grasp. The man screamed in terror and tried to run, but it was little use. Angela landed in a crouch, cast a quick concerned look towards O'Fallon, then an ugly one back to her prey. She roared again, leaped forward, bounced off the wall of a building and landed in the path of the escaping sailor. He skid to a stop and swung a savage, terror-driven punch at her head, which missed. She grinned and threw herself at him, pummeling the sailor and venting days upon days of pent-up terror and rage.

At the clearing, Hunter struggled to his feet, hissing in pain at the burn from his wounds. He had taken one step towards Angela and O'Fallon when something heavy immediately slammed into his back, nearly bending him backwards in two. The captain fell hard to the ground, devoid of air. He coughed, wheezed, then gasped, but could not get his breath. Rough hands jerked him onto his back. Suddenly, RiBeld was kneeling over him, punching him in the face.

Each punch slammed Hunter's head against the hard, packed ground. Once Hunter was dazed, RiBeld eased up and reached over for his knife that lay on the ground.

"You were supposed to find the children and then have the good grace to be too stupid to defend yourself when we attacked, then die!" RiBeld growled, his temper far outstripping his aloof, cold veneer.

Hunter tried to blink through the fog in his mind before he grinned ghoulishly through cracked and bloodied lips. "Or perhaps ... you are just that inept?"

Seething with rage, RiBeld backhanded the captain of the *Brass Griffin* and shifted his weight to pin Hunter's arms down. Because of the poor angle and the wounds both men suffered, he was only partially successful in trapping Hunter's right arm, but not his left. The mercenary captain jabbed down with the blade. Hunter managed to catch the cloth of the man's sleeve with his clockwork hand inches before the sharpened tip of RiBeld's knife could pierce skin. Gears protested at the abuse, but nonetheless held firm.

RiBeld glanced at Hunter, then Hunter's clockwork hand. "I'll dare say you'll lose more than a hand this day. You have been a right proper boil on my backside! One that I intend to lance!"

"Since ... you've already failed to do so ... why would you be ... competent enough ... to do it now ... Sirrah?" Hunter wheezed between gasps for air, struggling against the slowly descending knife.

"Your crew is lost. Your ship has been sent burning in the aether. You're just delaying the inevitable! Children and Heroes ... they die all the same! Alone!"

Explosions filled the air with fire and noise. The ground shook and buildings trembled while a screaming, tangible terror raced like a wild animal through the dirt streets of the village and into everyone there. Two buildings at the outer edge of the village had collapsed in on themselves as steaming grapeshot rained hot deadly metal on mercenaries and Yeti alike. Overhead, RiBeld's airship moved closer, her gunnery crews already preparing for another volley.

"Your people!" Hunter exclaimed incredulously while he struggled to keep the knife from his throat.

"Are... expendable! Any that are intelligent enough to find a way to survive I'll promote immediately." RiBeld answer him coldly. "You're lost. There's nothing left! Now why won't you and your cheap heroics die!"

The second volley fired upon the village. Immediately, that explosion of fire was followed by a second, then a sharp crack of lightning. Above, a bloom of fire erupted on one side of the massive airship. In shock, RiBeld and Hunter looked upwards, their own fight forgotten for the moment. There, rising behind and to the side of the mercenaries now-burning airship, the glint of the waning sunlight shone on brass and steel as the *Brass Griffin* soared up and around. Her lightning cannons fired, and high pressure salt water - powered from an airship's pump and charged by her store of batteries - tore huge gouts in the larger vessel's dark, nearly black hull. What the deadly lightning spared, the smaller cannon, filled with hot scrap metal shards, did not.

Using the momentary distraction, Hunter shifted to the right and let RiBeld's knife fall just beside his neck. He then changed his grip and latched onto RiBeld's wrist with his clockwork hand. The artificial fingers tightened, then locked into place with a dull grinding of tiny, protesting gears. Somewhere, deep within it, a spring popped angrily free with a sharp twang.

"Because Sirrah ..."

The captain squeezed his metal fingers and twisted. A series of pops, like wet sticks being broken, echoed in the air while arm bones just above the right wrist snapped cleanly in two. RiBeld's eyes and mouth went wide and his face ashen. He wanted to scream, to cry out. Pain clutched at his throat and refused him a single sound. The man struggled frantically, which allowed Hunter enough room to get a leg free. He savagely rammed a knee into RiBeld's groin with a angry growl.

"We're not nearly done!"

Chapter 16

Mushrooms of fire vomited from the mercenary's airship with each new cannon blast from the *Brass Griffin*. Hot, bitter smoke burned the air as explosions reached out with fingers of flame. They brushed - but never quite touched - the swift *Griffin* that screamed alongside its larger prey. Aboard her the crew cheered like madmen at each successful volley, exuberant at being able to pay back the mercenaries for just a little of the pain they had caused.

Krumer leaned on the railing to peer out at the larger craft after another explosion rocked both ships. "Damage report!"

A gunner raised his goggles and ran an appraising look over their large target. "She's burning hard, Mr Whitehorse! We surely caught'em wit' their trousers about their ankles!"

Krumer nodded in agreement. A savage grin brushed across his face, accented only by the wild spark that danced behind his eyes. Despite his usually calm demeanor, it was at moments such as this he felt the encouragement of ancestral war drums in his ears, calling him to battle. "Very good! Any other sign?"

"Aye! Fightin' below! These buggers are still trying ta butcher and barrage the village! Men, women, they're sparin' nothing!"

"Damnable monsters," Krumer growled. "They'll pay for each pain they give!"

Unaware of Krumer's comment, the gunner continued, "They're at it tooth and nail... and... Ah see the Cap'n! He's givin' some 'ristocrat what for!"

"It'll be RiBeld! Its gotta be who the Cap'n has got his hands about!" Tonks shouted.

Cheers deafened Krumer's attempt to reply, and eventually he gave up and let the crew have their moment. Fortunately, the impromptu celebration lasted only briefly. He moved to where he could face most of the main deck from the stairs that raced up towards the quarterdeck.

"Right then! If the Captain's below in the mix of this, we'll need to lend him a hand!" The first mate looked over his shoulder towards the wheel where Tonks stood. The pilot was like a statue. He stood, legs braced and hands firmly on the wheel, with a look of hard stone.

"Mr Wilkerson!" Krumer shouted.

"Aye!"

"Make for another pass!" Krumer ordered, and looked down the line of cannons and crew. For the non-lightning cannon, the two person crew rushed to pour more scrap metal into warm, copper bound iron cannon barrels. Once loaded, the tethers for each were pulled to drag the cannon back into place. On the lightning cannon, while similar in outline, the process went much more differently. Their 'ammunition' was a hose and a set of insulated wires. The hose snaked off to a modest sized storage tank and the wires to a set of barrel-shaped batteries. The only delay was to wait for the charge to build up in the capacitors between each discharge of lightning.

Krumer shouted again, "Goggles down! Ready the cannons to fire at will! Find me the neck of that bloated beast! I want her taken to ground!"

The cheers and shouts of encouragement drowned out any further orders from the first mate. Not that they were needed - the crew knew their job well. On the quarterdeck, Tonks grinned and spun the wheel hard to the right. As if in answer, the *Griffin*'s bow rose and an angry howl of wind rushed through her rigging while she turned, ready for another slice at her prey.

The *Griffin* turned to face the rear of the mercenaries' craft and leveled out for another pass. A hum quickly rippled through the air along the main deck while the lightning cannon powered up. Rapidly, gunners loaded the normal cannon while a shout rose above the din. What with the noise it was a wordless cry, but the tone was understood. The cannon were ready to fire.

In rapid succession, flashes of light as bright as the sun erupted from each cannon, capable of turning the blackest night to the brightest day. Peals of thunder, like the wordless roar of an angry lion, shook the air with a force that could be felt like a physical push from a giant hand. With each crack of thunder came the rush of water and creak of wood as the deck beneath each cannon protested at being bent just slightly out of shape. Directed by the salty stream, bolts of electricity - each powerful enough to illuminate the village below - reached out like electric claws from the starboard side of the *Griffin* to rake another deep wound in RiBeld's ship. Explosions of wood and powder stores filled the air with heat and smoke. Undaunted, the *Griffin* sailed through, emerging from the other side like some angered phoenix rising from the flames. Behind her, a massive, burning gash had been savagely ripped in the mercenaries airship where a handful of cannon had been.

The *Griffin*'s crew cheered again, but the cheer was cut short as a pair of harpoons pierced the hull and tethered her to the larger airship. Rigging and framework shrieked in protest just before the mercenaries turned their own cannon skyward. Suddenly, the *Griffin* was hammered once, then twice by volleys of grapeshot from the remaining cannon. The ship shuddered at the impact, scattering many of the crew from their feet and across the deck, battered and bloodied.

Despite wood splinters that flew through the air around him, Tonks held his stance at the wheel through the barrage. Near him at the stairs to the quarterdeck, Krumer likewise managed to keep his footing. The first mate looked down the twin lines of rope attached to the harpoons in horror as he saw a strong pair of steam-powered winches slowly drawing the *Griffin* closer. Beyond the winches, those of RiBeld's crew not operating the cannons brought up bundles from below. These were unwrapped so that swords, pistols, daggers or rifles could be handed out.

Krumer's own hand dropped instinctively to his waist to feel for his pistol while he shouted, "All hands! Cut those lines and repel all boarders!"

Far below, fires from the initial bombardment still burned angrily at ruined buildings and foliage. Smoke turned and swirled while

Yeti and mercenaries fought for control of the village. Slowly, the Yeti had begun to gain ground. In the clearing, Hunter released his metal grip on RiBeld's ruined wrist and shoved him aside. The mercenary leader whimpered in pain, then slowly rolled toward a nearby pistol, insane anger and agony in his eyes.

Hunter struggled to his knees, his vision slightly blurred from pain and sweat. There was movement a few feet away to his left. He wiped the sweat from his eyes in time to see RiBeld. Immediately, the captain reached for his pistol, but remembered too late that his holster was empty. He looked around and saw a pistol lying on the ground no more than four feet from him. As Captain Hunter started to lunge for it, he saw RiBeld raise his gun from the ground where he lay.

"No, oh no. You will not." RiBeld said in a pain-wracked, hoarse voice. "You will remain where you are, Sirrah. When I kill you, I shan't want to miss this time."

Hunter looked again at the pistol only four feet away. At that moment, it might have been four hundred for all the good it could do him. He tried to swallow but found his throat dry as sandpaper from the harsh mix of smoke, cold air and burning buildings. The captain sighed and kept his hands at his waist in plain view. "Answer a question for me then, Sirrah."

"Why should I bother?" RiBeld snarled.

"As you hold a gun on me, it would be the request of a condemned man. If that's not enough, then simply why not? You've nothing to gain or lose by answering one question."

RiBeld considered that a moment then slowly, painfully slowly, shifted to kneel on one knee. A smug, superior smile slowly crept over his face. "For a condemned man, I would grant your request. I am willing to allow you at least that in your last few moments."

Hunter's jaw clenched slightly. "You're too kind. My question is simple. Why my crew? Why were we so important in all this?"

RiBeld shrugged. "Two reasons. First, you did come highly recommended as both reliable merchant marines and privateers. Von Patterson felt you and your lot could locate the children among these forsaken mountains. Once their bodies were returned, there would be an outcry. Inquiries would be made. The Royal Navy is not stupid, as you well know, Sirrah. So a villain would be needed. Someone the Royal Navy would have little trouble in suspecting of ill-doing. Who better than one who was once one of their own. Namely you."

Hunter clenched and unclenched his fists slowly. "They would not accept that."

"With bodies they quite likely would. Namely those of the children and your crew. Though while some of the dead bodies of your crew would be produced and paraded about, you were to be barely alive. After all, they'd need someone to hang while Von Patterson expressed his deepest sorrow."

Hunter's face turned a light crimson, his fists clenched so tight that the skin stretched over his knuckles turned white. He rushed forward, intent to knock the gun from RiBeld's hand then beat the man into submission. However, Hunter only managed a few steps. RiBeld raised the pistol and cocked the hammer as he carefully got to his feet. "Ah, now that would be foolish. Though, I tire of Von Patterson's games. He'll have to make do with your body, as well. I've learned, to my dismay, that you and your crew are far too dangerous to leave alive.

It has been quite an adventure Captain Anthony Hunter. Farewell, Sirrah."

RiBeld squeezed the trigger. The hammer fell sharply but there was no smoke, no thunderous sound. Worse yet for RiBeld, Hunter did not fall to the ground. The gun had jammed.

"Curse you and your thrice-damned luck!" RiBeld threw the pistol and raced for the safety of the gap between buildings.

Hunter lunged for the pistol near him. He hit the ground in a roll, and came up to one knee, as he aimed at RiBeld's retreating back. Just when he made to pull the trigger, a shrill yell rang out to the captain's right that shattered his concentration.

"Captain!" Miles yelled, while looking around in terror yet clutching the opti-telegraphic. "I got it ta work! I can hear somethin' over it!"

Hunter glanced at the boy, then at RiBeld who was tensed to run at the child. Sensing Hunter's uncertainty, RiBeld ran at the boy and jerked him from his feet. Miles screamed in terror. Hunter aimed, but stayed his hand at pulling the trigger. Using the boy as a shield, RiBeld backed away slowly.

"You won't fire Hunter, I know you too well. You won't risk the boy's life!"

Steady, despite his wounds, Hunter leveled the pistol with his right hand at just below Miles' leg. Right in the area of RiBeld's left leg. "Indeed, Sirrah. I might not." He replied. "Unless I was certain of my shot."

Before he could squeeze the trigger, a flash of pain and lights exploded around Hunter's eyes. RiBeld's first mate, Johanssen, tossed aside the broken timber he had just clubbed Hunter with. Captain Hunter collapsed into the dirt, dazed.

RiBeld nodded and handed the screaming Miles to Johanssen. "Good man. Take this. It's time we left."

"Ja. Und de other one?"

"We only need the body of one child. We can let these primitives and nature finish his sister off."

"Ja, Captain."

With Miles screaming like a siren, the two men raced off between the buildings. From around another corner Moira and Angela appeared. It was Angela who saw her brother first.

"Miles!" She roared in a near panic.

Moira caught her before she raced off in one of her bounding jumps. "Na runnin' off! They'll be gunnin' ya down. 'Sides Ah might be gettin' 'em from here." Moira drew one pistol and took careful aim, calculating wind, smoke and the chaos of things that spun around her. She squeezed the trigger, the pistol bucking in her hand.

Instantly, Johanssen jerked, bits of clothing erupting from his back right shoulder. Despite that, he kept running, though not as fast. Moira swore harshly. "He must be havin' somethin' under that shirt. It should'a been droppin' him. Though he won't be gettin' far winged like that."

"Moira ... Angela ..." Hunter croaked hoarsely. Slowly, once more, he hauled his pain-wracked body off the ground.

"Cap'n!" Moira started to run over but Hunter waved her away.

"They are making their way to the longskiffs. They want us to chase them through that mess. Better to cut them off. We'll go around."

Angela kept glancing in the direction her brother had vanished, then back to Hunter who looked very beaten and battered. Finally she rushed over and helped the captain to his feet. Once he was upright, she released her hold on him. Her paw-like hands came away bloody from his wounds. "You shouldn't go. You're really hurt."

"The girl's speakin' some sense. O'Fallon's back under one o' them Yeti healers agin', faith knows where William be at by now. Ah'm na keen on ya bleedin' all out."

Hunter scowled darkly. "Then pray tell, do not watch. That monster and his band of hobgoblins have been trying to kill these children from the start and blame the murder upon us. Now they have Miles, despite my best efforts to prevent such. My wounds hurt dearly, but had they been more serious I'd not have survived the beating I had taken after being shot. Now I'm going after him. You can join me or watch as I half-run and half-limp around that devil's trap to catch him hopefully unaware."

Moira deftly opened the cylinder on her pistol and reloaded. "Ya always did be givin' the prettiest speeches. The moment we be loose o' this trouble, yer goin' to Doc and yer doin' whate'er he says. Agreed?"

"As we've little time to argue, I agree."

"Well then, lets be runnin' this fox ta ground for a' change."

Chapter 17

Captain Hunter and Moira ran, or limped in the captain's case, along the village paths. Angela, still in her werewolf form, bounded up and along a wall, then run off ahead. She would sniff the air, listen close, then return to report what she found.

The young girl stopped just ahead of Captain Hunter and Moira. "They 'ad laid a trap. I could 'ear several of 'em complainin' we 'adn't come along."

"Just like the man in thinking we'd bore straight after him. He has no tactical sense." Hunter growled, a hint of self-satisfaction in his tone. He then raised an eyebrow towards Angela, "Take deep breaths and mind your diction young lady. It's unbecoming."

"Yes, Sirrah." Angela's blush showed just slightly around her eyes from beneath her fur.

"Unbecomin'? Ah'd love ta be knowin' how?" Moira asked with a smirk.

Captain Hunter raised an eyebrow at her. "Not a word from you. You were harmed by too much time in the Americas."

Moira winked at Angela, then returned her attention to the matter at hand. "So Cap'n, how'd ya be knowin' about the trap? Ya never be sayin' ya met him afore." Moira asked.

"Correct, I have not. When you fight someone, you tend to learn a bit of their habits. Through that, a bit of themselves. He has no finesse. He's a rough brute at best. He may be a nobleman by birth, but by nature he's a base cad and a poor example of one at that." Hunter approached the corner of a building, glancing quickly around for any sign of ambush. Satisfied there was none, he motioned for the other two to follow. "This way is clear." Hunter paused with a sigh and turned. "Oh, pray tell, what is it Angela?"

Angela, who was quite literally, ever so slightly bouncing up and down on her hind paws, had a slight grin on her lupine features and a bright glint of excitement in her eyes. It was the look of any ten year old who had just discovered something important that no one else had yet learned. For a ten year old girl, the motion was distracting. In a ten year old werewolf girl, it was just short of disturbing.

"I think I'm knowin' ... pardon ... I know ... where Miles is! Right now! Right, right now!"

Both Moira and Hunter stopped dead in their tracks. "What? Where? Are we headed in the right direction?"

"Almost! A building more to the right and we'll be headed right for them! I can hear him yellin' in the trees."

Hunter had already changed his course to head in the direction Angela pointed. He called over his shoulder. "What else do you hear? Spare nothing, girl!"

The trio turned and raced along the cold, dirt path between mud-brick buildings, now scarred by bullets and blood stains. Angela maintained a running account of what sounds she heard.

"Clicking sounds. It's like a wheel. Now Miles is yelling again. Someone just yelled in pain." Her voice dropped an octave, an ugly feral snarl crept into her voice. "They're yelling at him again. Sayin' they're likely to hit him."

"Angela, concentrate."

She took two deep breaths. Slowly she regained her composure, though her anger still bubbled just beneath the surface of her thin calm. "Yes, Sirrah. I hear water and a whistle."

Moira cast a quick glance over at Angela while they ran. "A whistle? Like a shrill thing? Or be it a teakettle?"

Angela jumped over a forgotten bundle of ram fur with a single leap, then listened carefully again. "Teakettle."

"Cor blimey! They be at the longskiffs!"

"Steady, we'll get there."

Drawn to the noise of conversation, two mercenaries appeared with pistols drawn. One was dressed in gray trousers with a ragged cuff, a worn leather belt around his waist, a white shirt and an old brown vest. A day's worth of iron-gray stubble that matched his hair, adorned his face and chin. The other was dressed in a similar fashion: brown trousers instead of gray, no vest and and a malnourished, thin, reddish mustache instead of stubble. Both wore old black leather sailor's shoes that had seen better days. Their attitudes and swagger made it obvious they did not consider the badly wounded Captain Hunter, crouching Angela, or Moira a threat.

"Well 'ere now. 'ello me dear poppets." Said the one on the

right.

"We have no time for this, gentlemen. Stand aside." Captain Hunter warned the duo.

he one to Hunter's left giggled, very much like a young girl at play. A normal sound for a child. For an adult, it was very unsettling to hear. "Oh 'e sounds so purty. Me mate 'ere think ye more than enough time fer us, dearest!"

Hunter did not blink. He set his jaw, straightened his spine, and raised his hands slightly. All of this was merely a distraction that drew the sailors attention. Immediately, Moira sidestepped and aimed from her hip at the mercenary to Hunter's right. Angela burst from her crouch, jumped over to Captain Hunter's left side, then jumped again. Claws out, she slammed into the sailor on Hunter's left. The mustached sailor screamed in terror the moment Angela's blur resolved into an angry mass of fur and claws.

A few moments later, a smirk crossed Hunter's weary face while he limped by. He nodded to the wounded mercenaries, who now both rolled on the ground yelling in pain, clutching one or more shot or clawed appendages. "Word of advice gentlemen. When asked to stand aside for two fine ladies, one does so. Otherwise, said ladies, as you have noticed, take that rather ... poorly."

"It's Miles! He's yellin' again!" Angela exclaimed.

"Then we'd best hurry." Hunter replied.

Despite Hunter's wounds, they raced at best speed out of the village. Downslope in their direction, fingers of a dark tree line reached toward the village but did not quite touch it. Further down, the strands of trees joined together into a thick wash of greenery covered in the mountain snows.

No sooner than they had reached the first few thick stands of the snow-covered trees, a dull roar shook the air. Trees shivered from a blast of steam that rolled like a white wave through the branches. The wave of steam covered the trunks of the trees, fast turned to fog and engulfed Moira, Captain Hunter and Angela. Overhead, a longskiff rose quickly above the trees, its gas bag tight and main aft propeller already turning.

"No!" Angela screamed at the vessel, tears poured from her eyes and down along her snout.

Moira grabbed the girl by the shoulder to get her attention. "We're not done by half. There be another longskiff. We just need ta 'borrow' it a mite."

Captain Hunter limped quickly into the forest. "You can say 'take', I will not be offended."

"Usually ya be."

"Not today."

Deeper within the forest, beyond the thick stretch of trees that reached out toward the village, the second longskiff sat quietly in the snow. Two sailors were left aboard as sentries. At that moment, one was checking the boiler, while the other looked over the snow toward the trees.

"Are ye sure o' what the Cap'n said?"

The sailor at the boiler put down his wrench on a wooden bench in front of him. "Aye, ah'm sure. Three figures, says he. One woman, one girl and a man who's had the lovin' snot kicked outta him."

The sailor on watch shifted his sitting position. His face screwed up in thought. "That don' sound all bad."

A rush of wind blowing from the wrong direction and the faint scuffle of feet caught the lookout's attention. "Oi, Boyd, ye be hearin' that?"

There was no reply. The lookout frowned. He scanned the forest one more time, then turned around. "Boyd, be ye deef? Pay attention ..."

His words trailed off to a squeak when he saw his companion, Boyd, plastered against the railing of the longskiff. Atop his chest, Angela was perched with her claws pointed menacingly at a softer, more sensitive part of Boyd's anatomy. Namely, his throat. She growled at the lookout. "We need your boat!"

The sailor suddenly snapped out of his shock, struggling to jump up and bring his rifle to bear. He only made it off his seat when he heard the click of a gun being cocked not far behind him.

"I most certainly wouldn't try that if I were you, Sirrah." Captain Hunter advised while pointing his pistol at the sailor on lookout. "Now, Angela, manners young lady. Remember your manners."

Angela bared her teeth in a horrific mockery of a smile, and said in her most convincing ten year old little girl voice, "Please?" The lookout swallowed nervously and tried to smile in return. Slowly, he stepped from the boat.

Hunter limped toward the longskiff. "Ah, good man. The rifle, toss it away. Moira? Be a dear and check the boiler would you? It seems they had some trouble with it."

Moira grinned and holstered her pistol. "Aye, Cap'n. Gladly."

"Angela? I think the young man would like to join his friend."

Slowly, Angela climbed off her captive. The moment she was two steps away from him, he scrambled to his feet in a panic and nearly threw himself from the longskiff into the snow. Meanwhile, the lookout had fingered his rifle nervously, but had not thrown it aside.

Hunter limped closer. "I may have had the 'snot kicked out of me' but from this distance, Sirrah, I shan't miss any part of you I wish to put a large hole through before you raise that rifle. How dearly do you wish to suffer pain today? I'm in a right royal mood to assist."

With a sigh, the lookout tossed the rifle a good six feet from him into the snow. Captain Hunter smiled to the man.

"That's much better. Now, if you two gentlemen will excuse us, we'll be on our way."

Once aboard, Captain Hunter limped behind the wheel and throttle controls for the boiler. Moira looked over the steam engine, turbine, boiler and all the fittings.

"Lines be lookin' fair and fit. We can be castin' off. Just let me at the wheel and ah'll take her up."

"I've the wheel. See if this thing has an opti-telegraphic or something close aboard."

Moira hesitated a moment. Hunter raised an eyebrow.

"Problem, Ms Wycliffe?"

Moira stepped back and shook her head. "None at'all Cap'n. Checkin' for that Opti now."

She turned to look while the longskiff lifted abruptly from the ground. Angela joined Moira in searching.

"Isn't he too hurt to do that?" Angela asked in a whisper.

Moira nodded slightly. "Quite likely so. But he's got that look in his eye."

"What look?"

Moira looked cautiously at Captain Hunter, who did not notice, then shook her head just slightly. "Oh sweet peach, it be a look o' fire and brimstone in his eye. He set himself ta guardin' the two o' you and that RiBeld went and spit all over his honor by takin' ya brother among whatever else he said. Now he'd be chasin' RiBeld across Purgatory with a wet stick and a bucket o' sand till he be gettin' yer brother back." She gave Angela a reassuring smile. "Ah've seen him take four bullets and keep goin' till his job be done. If'n anyone can be gettin' yer brother back, it'd be him. Now, lets be findin' that Opti."

The pair searched what few components and controls that surrounded the boiler and steam engine itself. Finally, Moira pointed at an inset panel on a box that seemed out of place next to the boiler steam gauge. "Here, turn that knob."

Angela did so and suddenly the air was filled with Miles' panic-stricken voice.

"Hello? Hello? I know this works. I made it work. Someone's gotta hear me."

"Miles!" Angela screamed at the wooden and brass box.

"Angela? Angela!" Was the immediate sobbing reply.

Suddenly, both siblings were talking, sobbing and shouting over each other. Neither one was calm enough to wait for the other to speak. Finally, Moira interrupted.

"That'll be enough from both of ya. Miles, where'd they'd put you?"

"I dunno. They tossed me aboard a small boat. Then I tried to run after I kicked the man in the long coat in the shins." Miles repressed a nervous sniffle.

"Stout lad." Hunter commented tersely from behind the wheel.

Moira ignored Hunter. "Then what?"

"They grabbed me again and threw me in a box. I'm on the little boat. Kinda. Maybe. I dunno." His voice cracked, as if he was on the edge of sobbing again.

Moira leaned toward the opti-telegraphic mounted on the longskiff. "Ah, now, none o' that. Anyone who'd be able to get that wreck o' an Opti workin' with barely anything at all save what he be havin' on him shouldn't be sobbin'. Now did they say where they be headed?"

"The big ship. I heard 'em say it."

"Right then, you stay put as best as ya can. We're comin' for ya now."

"Ok. I gotta go. I didn't wind this up that much."

Moira nodded, even though there was no way Miles could see her. "All right, we'll be there soon."

There was no response however, save static.

Moira looked at Captain Hunter. He spared a glance over at Moira, then back to the skies where the bloody, explosive battle between the airships was taking place.

"They had ta know what he had with him." Moira commented.

"Of that I've no doubt." Hunter replied flatly.

"So they wanted us to talk to Miles?" Angela asked, a touch of confusion in her voice.

Hunter nodded. "That they did, my dear."

"But ..."

Moira answered her question before she spoke it. "A trap. They're plannin' on a trap o' some kind. Lettin' Miles natter his head off at us be the bait."

Angela looked between Moira and Captain Hunter. "So what do we do?"

The hint of a dark, mischievous nature touched Captain Hunter's face. "We spring it. And then burn it down around his noble ears."

Hunter spun the wheel sharply. The longskiff banked hard to starboard until its bow pointed directly for the mercenaries' burning airship.

Chapter 18

Not far above Captain Hunter's borrowed longskiff, a chaos of gunfire and swordplay echoed across the *Brass Griffin*'s deck. With the tethers firmly attached, the *Griffin* had been drawn close enough to the mercenaries' airship for two boarding parties of sailors to swing over and board her. Blasts of orange fire erupted from the bow, followed by deadly showers of bullets that peppered men and ship alike. Some of the crew fell in the volley of gunfire, but many stood their ground. Smoke burned eyes, smudged skin. Small fires burned in different places on the deck and rigging. Everywhere the faces of both crews took on the ghastly pallor of desperate men fighting for their ships, and therefore, their lives.

Close to one of the tether lines, Krumer lashed out with his cutlass. His intended target, a younger man in tight black cotton trousers, boots, white shirt and an elegant blue vest laughed and danced aside. The man was an elf, as was evident due to the slight graceful point of his ears and the distinctive arch of his eyebrows over his amber eyes. He spun like a well-trained dancer, his long, braided pony tail flowing behind him. Despite the air of grace and poise about the elf, the light in his eyes was wild and insane. Krumer's look, in contrast, was one of mild amusement mixed with irritation at the insulting fop in front of him.

"Come Orc! Surely someone taught you to use that blade better than one uses a butter knife!"

The elven fop completed his spin, only to find the point of Krumer's sword stuck through the fabric of his expensive vest, and into the wood behind him. Krumer grinned, then hammered a massive, well-tanned right fist into the fop's face once, twice, then a final time. Punch-drunk, the elven fop swung his rapier in a wild slice. Krumer let go of his own sword and neatly sidestepped the poor attack.

Then, he raised his fists and adopted a pugilist's stance. "Why no. But I did manage to learn a little when I took to boxing for a year in London." The fop started to reply and raise his sword, but Krumer interrupted that conversation with two fast jabs from his left, followed by his right, which hit the elven fop like a sledgehammer. Lips split, the elf's head rocked back and forth twice before he slowly oozed down the wood to the deck. With a chuckle, Krumer yanked his cutlass from the wood and turned away from his unconscious opponent.

Across the deck, the pitched battle had taken its toll on both sides. However, with a third of the mercenaries' crew on ground and a third having to man the guns and ship, that only left a third to try and cram themselves aboard a vessel half the size of their own. They simply could not get enough numbers past the *Brass Griffin*'s crew to subdue the smaller vessel.

"Push 'em back, lads! We're taking the fight out of them!" Krumer shouted.

The first mate waded into the mass of blades and chaos. Eventually, Krumer made his way to one of the tethers at the railing.

With a quick succession of slices, the first mate frayed the braided leather and let the pull of the *Griffin* do the rest. The first tether snapped with a loud pop and fell away. The ship shuddered, as if relieved to be free off one of her burdens. On deck, with raw, bloody determination, the crew finally pushed the mercenaries back to their own vessel.

From the bow, a shout rose over the fighting. "It's the Cap'n!"

Tonks and Krumer, both looked around in the direction the crewman had indicated. Krumer's grin broadened. "Ah, it's good to see him alive and breathing."

Tonks shook his head with a dark look, then pointed higher above Captain Hunter's longskiff. "Look above. He'll not be that for long."

From the far side of the larger airship, three steambats arced up, then banked hard. It was obvious that their target was not the partially tethered *Griffin*, but the longskiff!

Immediately, Krumer sheathed his cutlass in his belt and strode across the deck to recover a fallen rifle. "Not if we give them something more interesting to chew upon."

The first mate checked his load, aimed and then fired. However, the three steam-powered biplanes continued to arc and dive on the longskiff. Krumer reloaded and fired again, then again.

"Don't waste the ammo!" Tonks shouted. "They're outta range!"

"I'll not just stand by and do nothing!" Krumer shouted back angrily.

Tonks glanced at the trio of steambats, then back at the longskiff. Already the steambats had opened fire. Bullets and electrified jets of salt water reached angrily for the slower-moving longskiff. Bits of wood peppered and flaked off its hull. While his eyes measured the distance, a smile grew on the pilot's face as inspiration dawned on him. He grinned at Krumer. "Ya want your shot? I've got an idea that'll give it to ya!"

The first mate gave the pilot a curious look. "What would that be?"

Without warning, Tonks spun the wheel hard, turning the *Griffin* away from the mercenaries' airship. Unprepared, Krumer flew off his feet, then onto his backside. Before he could right himself, Krumer, along with several of the crew, slid wildly across the deck and slammed into the starboard rail, crashed into barrels, and smashed through crates that lay within their path. The *Griffin* strained and pulled at the single tether, which stretched so taught that the *Griffin*'s port side hull buckled outward from the tension. Tonks struggled with the wheel and trim controls. Slowly, amid the *Griffin*'s creaks and groans of stressed rigging and damaged structure, she turned her bow in the direction of the steambats and the longskiff.

The muscles on Tonks' arms bulged and his face turned red while he struggled to keep the *Griffin* aimed where he wanted. From the port side, the creaking rose in intensity to nearly a panic-filled shriek of strained wood and brass fittings. The winch at the other end of the tether pulled mercilessly, stretching the braided leather leash until it visibly grew thinner.

Krumer got to his knees and rubbed his head where he had

collided with a barrel. "Tonks! What in all the spirits are you about? Have you completely slipped your cog?"

Tonks squeezed his eyes shut and replied through clenched teeth. "Don't have time ta explain. Just cut the bloody tether afore we rip in two!"

Krumer had known Tonks for many a year. His tribal instincts screamed at him to run away, that his own life was in danger from whatever Tonks had in mind. However, Krumer trusted Tonks. He had known him too long to believe the man would needlessly put their lives in danger. Scrambling to his feet, Krumer raced as best he could across the slanted deck to grab a forgotten axe embedded in the mast. The orc jerked that free, then at the port railing swung the blade over his head. For a moment, the sunlight glinted off the metal of the weapon before Krumer bellowed an ancient war cry of his people. With one powerful slice, the axe severed the braided leather line that was, even stretched, nearly as thick as a man's arm.

The tether cracked like a whip in the air and snapped backwards towards the winch on the other ship. Released from the leather leash, the *Griffin* shot forward with a shriek from strained planks and wind tossed rigging. On deck, the crew clung to the rail, rigging, tied down barrels, anything stable. When she launched forward, Krumer had been thrown clear across the deck again, this time against the steps to the quarterdeck. Slowly, he righted himself and ascended the ladder.

"I trust you know what you're about!" Krumer shouted over the high winds.

Tonks had stood again, but his eyes were riveted on their new course heading - right between the steambats and the longskiff. "Aye, that makes the both o' us! We'll only get one shot here! Make that broadside a' good one!" The pilot took a deep breath to steady a brief twinge in his nerves. "Comin' in fast. Steambats on the port side! Gunners better get ready!"

On the quarterdeck now, Krumer clutched rail next to the ladder and took a deep breath before he bellowed to the main deck. "Goggles down! To your cannons! I want those 'bats out of our sky!"

The main deck came alive like an anthill with his orders. Crew members - both the lightly wounded and the lucky few still unharmed - raced or limped to the left side of the *Griffin* and muscled cannon into place.

"Comin' in steep!" Tonks called out. "Arrivin' in ten, nine ..."

Shouts echoed the call on the main deck. Gunners braced for the moment while the hum of lightning cannons filled the air like a swarm of enraged bees.

"... three, two, one!"

Krumer slammed his right fist against the railing. "Fire broadside! Fire! Fire!"

At the first mate's command, each cannon shook, then spit fire and lightning. The left side of the ship erupted with a bright, intense light as the thunderous roll of cannon vibrated the very air. White-hot scrap metal and streams of salt water, overcharged with electricity, reached out to clutch at the fast moving steambats with a hungry intensity. For the trio of steambat pilots, realization came to them at the last moment when the *Griffin* shoved across their path, much faster than she should have been able to. Frantically, they tried to bank, to turn. To be anywhere but where they were right at that moment. However, the *Griffin* was bent on protecting her missing crew in the longskiff. She was not to be denied. The steambats erupted in balls of canvas, steam, wood and brass. Their debris rained down around and on the *Griffin*.

Just a few yards below the *Griffin*, her captain sailed past with as much speed as the longskiff could manage. He saw the exchange above, and despite an involuntary wince at the strain he just knew had happened to his ship, he wanted to salute and smile at the ingenuity of his crew. At that moment, however, he had larger issues to concern himself with.

"I'm losing starboard control, Moira! We're listing badly! Pray tell, what did we lose?" Hunter called out while he fought with the wheel.

Moira, with Angela in close tow, scrambled to the right side and peered over. While a longskiff was held aloft by an appropriate-sized gas bag, it was only the means of lift, not propulsion. On the rear and just below the line of sight there were three propellers - one large and two small - and a small set of fins. The large propeller provided the main means of forward motion, but the fins and smaller propellers could tilt and adjust. These allowed the pilot to fine tune the direction or turn. At that moment, only the main propeller, fin and smaller propeller for the left side of the small boat were functional. The smaller right propeller hung at a crazed angle and the small right fin had been snapped cleanly in the middle.

Moira leaned back up and looked at Captain Hunter.

Hunter struggled with the wheel and frowned. "Well?"

Moira exchanged a worried look with Angela then they both leaned back over the side at the damage. The two ladies then leaned back into the longskiff. Moira looked around, a bright glimmer in her eyes. "It's na gone."

Hunter's frown darkened. "What? How do you mean?"

Angela bit her lip and looked over the side again. Moira's eyes settled on running boards, stowed oars and other parts of the longskiff. "Ah can be fixin' it."

The young werewolf girl sat up straight and stared aghast at Moira. "What?"

Hunter raised an eyebrow suspiciously but reserved his comments, since the longskiff chose that moment to fight him again while they passed beneath the *Griffin*. "Good."

Moira turned towards Angela. "And Ah'll be needin' yer help."

Angela's eyes grew wider. She pointed at the side with the damage just when the longskiff jerked on the wind. "But ... it's danglin' ..." she said in a small voice.

The blacksmith ignored the girl's protests and looked around the longskiff. "Aye, aye. We'll be needing somethin' fer that." Moira pulled loose one of the plank seats, snatched up spare rope, and grabbed an emergency hatchet. Again the blacksmith cast about the boat for anything loose.

"Moira... the fan thing." Angela stammered when another groan of metal escaped the wounded machinery.

"Aye, it be called a 'screw', sweet peach." Moira answered

quickly while she checked the rope for any frayed spots.

"It's ... danglin'. I think it's goin' to fall. How're we going to fix somethin' like that?"

Moira frowned and looked over the side at the damaged section. She sat up and glanced over her loose collection of random parts in front of her. Without another thought, she opened a small panel in a small box next to the opti-telegraphic then yanked out a long bundle of wires. Angela jumped as if shot and stared in horror at what Moira had done.

She presented the batch to Angela, "That's what we'll be usin'."

The girl looked at the box, then the wires. She shook them slightly at Moira. "Don't we need these for something important?"

Moira shook her head. "Na a bit. Those be for a backup, emergency battery. We can be missin' it for a bit. Now hold on a moment." With a savage swing, Moira slammed the hatchet down against the longskiff bottom and severed the rope she had found in two.

She handed one end to Angela. "Hand me what Ah'll be askin' for, when Ah call out."

Angela whimpered slightly, but eventually sighed then nodded.

Suspended by a tenuous balance on the rail with her foot hooked under a wooden seat plank, Moira fashioned a makeshift splint by lashing the wood to the broken fin with the remains of the rope. The wires she used to repair frayed connections to the propeller and lash the housing of the screw to a set of twisted bolts that protruded from the hull.

Moira leaned back up just as the longskiff bounced once more, jostling its occupants. Crude as the repairs were, the damaged screw sputtered, hummed, then began to spin. In moments, the little boat steadied out, despite the high winds and occasional bullets or debris that fell past. Moira brushed her hands together with a satisfied smile.

"That'll do 'er, Cap'n! Least till Ah can be gettin' get at it proper with tools and more a few bits and pieces."

Captain Hunter nodded. A smile of approval appeared briefly on his face while he navigated the perilous route through the aerial combat around them. "Excellent, as we are about to land. Though I fear it may be a bit ... steep."

This time it was Moira's turn to look stunned. "What?"

Behind her, Angela, turned to look in the direction they were headed. Abruptly, she let out a shrieking howl of surprise and terror. Moira spun around as Angela cowered against her, eyes closed.

"What be the noise?" The rest of Moira's words caught in her throat when she saw where they were.

The longskiff had sailed directly underneath the *Brass Griffin*. From there they had turned to move between the *Griffin* and the mercenaries' larger airship! Cannon and rifle fire flew between the two in bursts of deadly light. The yells and cries of pain from both crews filled the air between the thunderous boom of cannon and staccato crack of rifles. Bullets and lighting crisscrossed the air to form a lethal net.

Just beyond the deadly display, the landing harness for the mercenaries' airship took shape out of thick clouds of bitter smoke. A steambat aircraft waited in the cradle of leather for the pilot to slide the craft out into the air. The small craft's propellers spun as the steam engine boiled to life, pulling the canvas and wood craft into the air, then directly into the path of a stream of lightning from the *Brass Griffin*. High pressure jets of water hammered the canvas structure, and lightning played violently across the brass fittings of the engine. Wires melted, canvas burned and metal pipes deformed then broke away from their fittings. No more than a moment after her launch, the steambat turned her nose down and fell the ground below.

"That's where we'll board her!" Hunter shouted over the chaos.

"There?" Moira looked from the landing harness to the smoke and fire beyond, then back to Captain Hunter.

"Yes, there. We're only ten feet above where we need to be. Just have to bring the 'skiff down a touch."

Moira wiped a grease-stained hand across her face and let out a shuddering sigh. "Oh ... my. Cap'n's at the helm." The blacksmith joined Angela in closing her eyes.

Hunter let the shade of a grin touch his lips before he pulled a cord to slow-vent the air of the gas bag and hit the emergency stop lever on the longskiff's engine. "Indeed."

The small craft shuddered, as the engine stopped. Abruptly, the boat dropped sharply towards the net.

Chapter 19

With air escaping the gas bag and the longskiff's steam engine no longer powering the propeller, the small airship hurtled downward. Hunter clutched the engine controls with a death grip. His eyes focused, unblinking, on the leather harness that rapidly drew closer with every passing second. Suddenly, he shoved a lever down. Sparks flew from the housing as the steam engine sputtered to life, powered by the longskiff's primary batteries. Two seconds later, the propellers roared to top speed and the longskiff leveled out.

The small airship struck the landing harness at full speed. Leather straps stretched and creaked horribly, but held against the impact and weight of the longskiff. Hunter threw the lever again to cut power to the steam engine. He pulled a cord to close the leak from the gas bag, leaving just enough air to give the longskiff some lift later, but not enough for it to float away.

Stray bullets shot by, and occasionally wood exploded into fragments while the longskiff swayed drunkenly in the landing harness. The motion soon settled to match the main airship. Captain Hunter drew his pistol, then looked over to check on his companions.

"All hale and whole?" He asked.

Angela nodded hesitantly, her eyes darting around in alarm at all the new sounds and smells threatening to overwhelm her young werewolf senses.

Moira sighed, and likewise nodded. "Aye, all parts be accounted for. Though, Cap'n, we've sprung their trap, how're we ta be findin' Miles?"

Hunter looked to Angela. "We'll need your help with that, my dear. We can try the opti-telegraphic but I've not any confidence he'll be able to see where they've put him to give us clues in finding him. Though you might could discern something."

Angela closed her eyes to concentrate. A moment later, she opened them, fatigue showing in her canine face. "It's so noisy..."

Moira shook her head slightly. "She's been through a ringer, Cap'n. Ah might can toss apart our opti-telegraphic, then be makin' a quick locator ta find Miles' opti?"

The young werewolf shook her head. "No, I can do this." She closed her eyes again and grabbed the railing with her paw-like hands. Her claws cut small grooves in the wood as she extended, then retracted them idly. Finally her eyes snapped wide open. She swayed a little, as if slightly dizzy.

Moira stepped forward to steady the young girl. "What do ya hear?"
"No ... " she said with a gasp, then shrieked, "Miles!" Abruptly, she launched herself over the rail. In one bound, she had leaped from the longskiff and across eight feet of the mercenaries' airship.

"Angela! Wait!" Captain Hunter swore, then hammered the

longskiff's railing with a fist. "Bloody hell and damnation! Don't lose sight of her!" He leaped over the rail and landed in a crouch on deck of the larger ship. Quickly, he raced off after Angela, with Moira not far behind him.

In a mad chase, Angela leaped and dodged across the deck, racing headlong towards her brother's terrified and angry shouts. Captain Hunter and Moira followed close behind as best they could. Not able to dodge as well as the young girl, they fired upon those sailors unfortunate enough to cross their path, or simply ambushed them along the way. Moira's shots were deadly and careful, with one per target. Hunter's less so, but what he missed with bullets, he occasionally resolved with a well-placed fist. When his latest pistol clicked on an empty chamber, he resigned himself to just his fists and wits.

While Angela was not entirely deaf or blind to any of this in her headlong search, her focus was mainly on her younger brother. His screams were like needles pricking her skin, grating her nerves with the anxiety that she was not there - yet - to protect him. Although, no matter how carefully she listened, the noise of the battle blurred the sounds the closer she got to where she believed he was. A desperate panic rose in her mind that clouded her concentration and threatened to overwhelm her completely. She needed information. She wondered how Hunter or Moira would find out. Then, she had an idea.

The young werewolf vaulted a trio of barrels and landed on an unsuspecting sailor. Pistol and sword fell from his grip and skittered across the deck. He started to rise, but as he did, she slammed her paws onto his back and leaned so close, the harsh rasp of her angry breath blew across one of his ears.

"Ye gods!" He yelped when realization dawned upon him as to just who - and what - was on his back.

"Where is my brother?" She demanded.

"Whot?" He squeaked then swallowed hard. He laughed nervously, then tried a half-hearted attempt to stall. "Ye gots a brother?"

"The young boy. Where ... is ... he? Tell me!" She snarled, a dark and ugly undertone creeping into her voice.

"W ... wait! The whelp's ahead! With the Cap'n!" The sailor pointed with a free hand towards the quarterdeck then licked his dry and cracked lips, his eyes wide in fear. "Narry a soul's ta touch 'im. Cap'n's orders! Ya let ... let me go, eh? Roit?"
"You'd better not be lyin'!"

"Ah'm swearin' it! On me muther's grave! If ... if she was in one ... bless 'er soul!" He stammered in a panic.

"All right. I'll let you go." Without another word, she sprung off the back of the sailor towards the direction he indicated. Behind her, the man squeezed his eyes shut and sighed heavily with relief.

A short race across the deck towards the rear, Angela jumped up onto a crate and crouched down. Just ten feet ahead she saw Miles. He looked only slightly the worse for wear, as he was more disheveled than before. He had been bound to the narrow railing that braced the side of the ladder to the ship's quarterdeck with a thick stretch of hemp rope. Archibald RiBeld was there, just retying the last knot on Miles' wrist. RiBeld's coat was torn. Dirt and blood smudged his fine linen shirt, and his hair tossed wild about him on the wind. He looked less the aristocrat and more an apparition from a nightmare. About him stood five armed men, none of whom had a pleasant look for Miles. When RiBeld was done, he grabbed Miles roughly by the chin.

"Now you little maggot, you'll not free yourself this time! Not if you know what's good for you!" RiBeld shook Miles by the chin then let go.

"Miles!" Angela yowled, heedless of the danger in front of her.

Miles' eyes went wide, fully aware of the trouble they were in. "Angela? Run away!"

"The shape shifting whelp! Excellent! My second catch of the day!" In a blur of motion, RiBeld yanked a pistol from one of the sailors near him and cocked the hammer.

Immediately a barrel arced down from above and slammed against the mercenary captain. Heavy wooden slats, abused by both weather and battle, broke apart on impact. RiBeld was engulfed in a cloud of splintered wood that knocked him off his feet and across the deck. His pistol flew into the air and over the side of the ship to the ground far below.

"Which means you've not read the notice, Sirrah. It says 'off limits'!" Hunter shouted as he reached for a second barrel despite the rising pain that rippled through him. Bullet wounds reopened, then tortured him with white-hot pain and dull aches for every abrupt movement. The pain quickly became a distraction, one that he knew he could not afford to focus on. With an extreme force of will, he concentrated on the moment. His pain he would think about later.

Off to Hunter's left, behind some crates, Moira rose up,

outlined by a bright fire burning several feet behind her. A pistol in each hand, she fired once, then twice. A look of cold fury glinted in her eyes with a deathly light. Ahead of her, as two sailors dropped like stones, the others scattered for cover like rabbits from a hawk.

RiBeld shook off the wood, then spit blood from his broken lip. He shot a look of pure acidic hatred at Captain Hunter. "You! Again! Always you!"

The nobleman turned mercenary got to his feet and grabbed one of his men. Deftly, he yanked the sword from the sailor's hand and shoved him directly into the path of Moira's guns. The sailor jerked twice and fell abruptly from the staccato sounds of gunfire intended for RiBeld. Without a concern for his fallen man, RiBeld stepped around the obstacle, roared like a wounded bear, then charged Captain Hunter.

Suddenly struck by cannon fire, the deck exploded to Hunter's right in a shower of smoke and hot timbers. As RiBeld rushed forward, Hunter looked around for a weapon, anything he could defend himself with. Next to him lay a dead sailor who had been killed by an explosion. The dead man's clothes and few personal possessions were obviously ruined, given his burned state. However, the sailor still had his cutlass. It had fallen beneath him during his last moments. Captain Hunter reached down, grabbed the sword and pulled. It was firmly pinned beneath the body and debris.

"Come on," Hunter said in frustration. He looked up, RiBeld shoved aside another crewman in his headlong tear across the deck. The mercenary yelled in rage while he ran, his eyes bright with murder, his face twisted and evil. RiBeld raised his sword higher the closer he came, the dying sunlight and reflected explosions shone blood red against the worn blade. Hunter bent harder to his task, braced a foot against the debris and pulled. The debris shifted and the sword began to move.

RiBeld shoved his way forward with a maniacal grin spread across his face. He raised his blade and leaped at his prey. In moments it would be finally over. He could sense it.

At the last moment, the cutlass came free and Hunter swung the blade upwards. It connected just before RiBeld's own blade could cause any harm. Both men pulled back, and RiBeld swung again. Hunter stayed on the defensive, blocking each blow in turn. Metal slid against metal, then scraped with a small shower of sparks as the two men glared at each other.

"These children leave this ship alive." Hunter snarled while he fought to shove RiBeld's blade aside.

"Fine enough. Once I dispatch you, they'll be simple enough to find. Though, I've more than enough crew to put an end to both your misfits and the 'lovely' cherubs!" RiBeld replied icily.

The ship pitched suddenly, and both men scrambled to keep their footing. Captain Hunter found enough of a foothold first, then shoved the mercenary leader away. RiBeld stumbled back ten feet and collided against a loose barrel due to the dramatic roll of the ship.

RiBeld struggled to his feet, then stopped dead in his tracks. Beyond Hunter, Angela had just sliced the ropes that bound Miles to the rail. Moira, with a satisfied smile, punched the last mercenary that had thought to keep them from Miles. The ropes pooled slowly onto the deck while Angela and Miles raced towards Moira. RiBeld was without dagger or a pistol. With only a sword, all he could do was watch while they raced for the clear path along the deck. His hastily contrived plan lay in ruins.

Moira waved encouragement to the children as they ran past her, then shouted, "This way! Cap'n! To the longskiff! Ah got 'em! Ah got 'em!"

Hunter nodded in their direction, then turned to face RiBeld. A smile tugged at the captain's face as he touched the hilt of his sword to his forehead in a fencing salute. "I, the misfits, and the cherubs bid you good day! May you go down with your worm-eaten, misbegotten ship!"

Fury exploded inside RiBeld as Hunter broke off the duel to race after Moira and the children.

"No!" RiBeld screamed, his fists shook with uncontrolled rage. "No!"

Rage boiled like a searing heat, consuming his every thought. He ran forward, searching, until he found one of his own men laying face down on the deck, quite dead. Roughly, he shoved the body over. RiBeld's anger quickly gave way to insane elation as he drew the dead man's pistol and aimed. "No, Captain Hunter, I bid you ... good day. I'll see you in hell!"

The pistol boomed then bucked in RiBeld's hand. No more than a second later, Hunter bent backwards, eyes wide in shock and pain from the impact of the bullet. He jerked from the force of the blow, stumbled, then lost his footing. Pitching forward, he slammed into a broken spar of wood with a heavy thud. Closer to the longskiff, the shot and sound startled Angela. Immediately she spun, the world slowing to a crawl while Hunter slid to the deck. Next to her, Miles and Moira came to a quick stop as well.

Miles screamed and launched himself towards Hunter, but Moira caught him before he took a step. Angela froze, eyes wide, unable to will herself to move. Across the deck, Hunter slowly shoved himself up and looked to Moira.

"Go!" He yelled hoarsely. Moira started to shake her head, but he cut her off. "Don't argue! The children come first!"

A long list of objections fought their way forward in Moira's mind. With a visible effort, she forced her objections back, then grabbed Angela by the shoulder. Hunter was right and she knew it. "Ya be hearin' the Cap'n! We gotta go!"

The touch of Moira's hand shook Angela from her shock. She screamed, and struggled to run towards Hunter. Moira stumbled, but managed to keep a firm hold on both children. With a last look towards the captain, she dragged them across the deck in a headlong run for the longskiff. Behind where they had stood, the deck planks exploded. Wooden shards clouded the air and peppered anything nearby.

Laying face down upon the deck, Hunter could hear RiBeld laughing. The man said something, but Hunter could not make a word of it. He assumed it was more gloating or death threats. At that moment, he honestly did not care. As he tried to invent a biting retort, an explosion shook the ship, ripping up the deck planks not far behind him. Hunter remained where he lay, paying the latest in what had seemed to be a long chain of destruction little heed. Too tired and wounded to fight, the captain waited for the inevitable - RiBeld's blade in his back.

Only the anticipated thrust never arrived. After a time, Hunter looked up again, but saw only smoke and haze around him. Fires burned here and there in ruined holes about the ship. Bent steam pipes thrust up at crazed angles, and torn rigging lay in numerous places. The clouds of smoke that played among the rigging and ran along the deck completed the hellish landscape. Slowly, he got his hands under him and pushed. White-hot pain lanced through his left shoulder like hot iron from a forge. He gasped and nearly fell, but managed to not plunge face-first against the deck.

Each inch he raised himself upright was a momentous accomplishment, until finally the captain managed to brace himself on one knee. He looked around, and to his amazement saw no one nearby. That was not to say the ship was abandoned. Far from it, as RiBeld's men were busy at the bow of the ship. Some were desperate to clear debris and save trapped comrades. Others emerged from below-decks with what few personal belongings they owned. By and large, they were abandoning ship. Captain Hunter looked around again. RiBeld was nowhere to be seen.

"I shouldn't be surprised at that." He grunted to himself. With a deep breath and slow, determined motion, Hunter rose unsteadily to his feet. The ship swayed and his knees threatened to buckle. Quickly, he leaned out to steady himself against the mast and get his bearings.

At that moment, a break in the smoke chose to appear. There, directly ahead of the rapidly descending airship, was the Yeti village! Hunter groaned and let out a sigh. It was a sharp, torturous experience, as it brought on a fit of pain from his shoulder. He had to raise the ship's heading, at least enough for the dying wreck to miss the village and crash harmlessly in the snowy mountainside beyond. As quickly as he physically could, he limped over to the nearby ladder and ascended. On the quarterdeck itself, exhausted and wounded, Captain Hunter's legs gave out from under him. He fell to the ship's deck barely a foot from the wheel, his blood forming a modest stain on the wood. He looked up at the short distance that remained and swore hoarsely at himself, then at the entire world before he tried once again to rise. Only this time, he failed.

Suddenly, from out of the hellfire landscape, familiar voices echoed in his ears. Hunter tried to call out, but his throat was raw from the smoke and all the punishment he had taken. His cry was weak, ineffective and unheard. Frustrated, angry, he located a stray piece of burnt wood and slammed it on the deck in a rapid pattern. A weak attempt to tap Morse code for 'SOS', at best. The sound of wood against wood echoed dull and dead in the air. Not long after, the furred shadow of a figure appeared at the top of the ladder behind Hunter.

"He's here! He's here!" Angela shouted, her voice thick and hoarse from gasping in smoke.

There was a scramble of footsteps and Hunter felt arms under his. "There Cap'n, Ah got ya." Moira said.

"I gave you an order ..." he began slowly, with smoke-dry mouth and tongue.

Moira interrupted him. "That ya did. But, bless her soul, the young miss be trottin' out a good point. Ya didna leave Miles ta RiBeld. Ya be stayin' by them through all this. So, she's makin' sure we be stayin' by ya in turn cause she be sayin' that someone needs ta watch over ya. After seein' ya now? Cor blimey, Ah'm agreein."

The captain started to say something harsh about the necessity to obey orders when lives depended on it. He decided, right then, it was not worth it. There were more important matters at hand. "Moira, the ship... the village..."

"Shush Cap'n, Ah laid me own eyes on it. Angela?" Moira called out.

"Yes, mum?" The girl replied from over by the wheel. She had adjusted the course slightly and slowly, very much in the fashion of someone unused to the sensations of piloting an airship.

"Course laid in?"

"Just like ya told me to, Moira. It should be missin' the village. I'm pretty sure, anyway." The young werewolf chewed her lip slightly from uncertainty.

"It'll have ta do. Come be helpin' meself and Miles with the captain. We don't have the time ta waste, no matter how ya slice it."

Angela reached up and yanked down some stray rigging which had been shot loose some time ago. Using that, she lashed the wheel in place, setting its final course out into the snow. Slowly, the ship began to turn, then rise to a path well above the Yeti village. That done, she raced over and helped the others maneuver the wounded captain. With her help, Moira pulled the captain to his feet. Unsteady, Hunter tried to walk, but exhaustion and blood loss had taken its toll. His knees gave way and he pitched headlong towards the deck with Moira in tow. Moira stumbled but kept her footing and her hold on the captain.

"Easy now Cap'n, steady as she goes." Moira reassured him.

Miles, desperate to help, tried to brace Hunter on the side opposite from Moira, but to little effect. Angela fared some better, but she was hampered by her smaller size with respect to the two adults. Moira smiled thinly and gestured for them both to back away.

"Ah can manage, though both ya hearts' are in the proper place. C'mon, we've little time. Ah doubt this bird's got much more ta keep her aloft." With that Moira guided Hunter down the ladder and led him and the children across the deck in a slow, but determined race against time.

Miles looked over at Moira when they were mid-way to the longskiff, "Moira?"

Moira glanced at Miles. "Yes, young Sirrah?"

"This mean we can be going home now? Maybe just someplace safe?"

Moira smiled as she helped Hunter past some ruined, charred debris. Ahead, their 'borrowed' longskiff loomed in the smoke, perched in the landing harness as though it could leap out and fly at any moment. This was provided the steam engine turbines were cooperating and had not been too badly damaged.

She nodded. "Yes, dear heart, it's past time ya both be goin' back ta ya parents."

At the longskiff, Moira eased the captain aboard. She sat him on one of the wooden seats but what with the exhaustion, Hunter chose to lay flat instead and closed his eyes. Moira climbed behind the controls. Miles and Angela scrambled in next. Miles sat next to the captain while Angela looked over the side at the makeshift repairs from earlier. She sat back and gave Moira a worried look.

"Cross ya fingers, sweet peach. Lets be seein' if she'll hold." Moira said while she looked over the controls. She took a deep breath, then pulled the lever for the battery. Sparks showered Moira, the engine coughed, churned, then sat still. Moira's blood ran cold.

"Battery leads ... " Hunter croaked while he fought back unconsciousness. "Check the leads. Odd smell when we landed ... something burnt ..."

"Of course!" Moira exclaimed, then dove down to yank open the battery panel. "Got me head all up in the clouds in the excitement."

Deftly, she followed the lead wires from the steam turbine and boiler to the brass and tempered glass battery that charged the heating plates for the boiler. Where the wires had at one time terminated at the battery, now there were charred ends. Moira swore and looked around at what was at hand. She eventually reached over to a collection of wires and tugged hard. Two strands popped loose, causing a valve needle to shake angrily on the console. These she spliced into the ignition wires and reattached to the battery.

"What was that?" Angela asked nervously, a worried look on her face.

"Nothin' too serious, sweet peach." Moira said as she wiped soot from her hands on her trousers. "Just borrowin' connection's from something else on the panel here."

Moira tugged the lever up, then pulled it down again. This time sparks flew, grayish gas trapped in the thin heating plate ignited, and the steam turbine came back to life while the boiler's steam pressure rose. The lady blacksmith smiled in satisfaction.

Angela was less than encouraged. "What'd those wires used to do?"

"Ah well... just for the secondary pressure gauge. We'll na be needin' that. The *Griffin*'s right over there. Trust me." Moira winked at Angela, fired the burner for the gas bag, and shifted the propellers on full speed. "We'll be back aboard there afore ya know it!"

Even though Moira was right, Angela still thought it the longest five minutes of her young life.

Chapter 20

Steam issued from the vents around the longskiff, pouring along the snow-covered grass and turning to a fog as white as a cloud. As the small vessel descended amid this cover, the cloud billowed up and around the occupants, then rose above the gas bag to spread on the wind. Tonks gently pulled the lever to vent some of the air from the gas bag and bring the propellers to a full stop before he let the small airboat come to rest on the cold, damp clearing. Across the level ground, one hundred yards to their right, another airship hovered several yards in the air anchored to a large post. Only a few feet longer than the *Brass Griffin*, she had the similar lines of a schooner, but with a second set of trim sails the *Griffin* did not have as well as a few more feet of cargo space, given the deeper draft of her keel. Beyond the schooner, an ancient walled town lay partially buried in the thick forests. The entire site sat nestled among the mountains, nine days' travel by airship from the reclusive Yeti village.

The crew of the other airship ship had been busy unloading boxes of cargo and supplies for the modest-sized tent village located outside the ruin. It was the campsite of an archeological expedition that had arrived some months prior. Rumors persisted that the ruins were the remains of a Roman colony formed from the remnants of a lost expedition that had gone in search of the legendary land of Thule. So far, based on the recovered artifacts that sat neatly arranged among the tents, the rumors were likely true. Unloaded boxes from the airship that stood waiting to be opened were all stamped 'Property of the British Museum' and 'Delivery to Von Patterson expedition' in bold, black painted letters. With the arrival of the *Griffin*, and the landing of the longskiff a few minutes later, most of the energy had turned from unloading to curiosity at the newcomers.

Hunter rose from one of the wooden seats and stretched. He winced at the pain from several wounds, now bandaged under a clean shirt and re-stitched long coat. Beside him, his traveling companions stirred as well. Angela and Miles, both scrubbed and dressed in cleaner clothes, looked around, eager to take in all the new sights and sounds. Moira joined them after a moment, as in awe of the surroundings as the two children. Behind her, the *Griffin's* doctor, Thorias, eyed the view skeptically.

Tonks tugged off his pair of worn leather pilots' gauntlets and pulled off his goggles. "Groundside, Cap'n. Looks like we'll be the center attraction for a bit."

The captain glanced over to Tonks. "Good piloting, Mr. Wilkerson. Although, I dare say they were just not expecting us."

Hunter leaned forward on his cane carefully to look around at the ruins and forest greenery. Curious for a closer view, he walked slowly over to the edge of the boat, stepping onto the now exposed brownish-tan carpet of grass that surrounded them. When Moira and Tonks moved to assist him, Captain Hunter frowned.

"I daresay that a retinue is not required for this. There are repairs to the *Griffin* that are still waiting attention." The captain said sternly.

As Thorias stood and stretched, Arcady - present on the doctor's shoulder as always - took flight to circle slowly about the crew. The doctor rubbed one of his gracefully pointed elven ears in hopes to clear the ringing he suffered from sitting too close to the small boat's steam turbine. He wore his long woolen peacoat as proof against the mountain chill and icy winds, however at times the cold still managed to seep in. He sighed faintly as the ringing in his ears was intent to stop in its own good time.

"It was doctor's orders you rest and leave this to Mr. Whitehorse. Naturally, though I don't know why I expected otherwise, you ignored that and came anyway. So, it's doctors orders you have a retinue. Perhaps - this time - you won't have anyone trying to shoot, stab or electrocute you to death." Thorias commented wryly and walked over to the side of the longskiff.

Hunter started to open his mouth to say something, but then thought better of it. He closed his mouth and sighed. Thorias had a point. He was supposed to be in his cabin, resting. Although, he had been confined to quarters and rest for the past nine days in their flight to the ruin. Deep down, though he refused to admit it openly, he was stark-raving bored.

Hunter leaned on his cane for momentary support. "That may very well be, however I gave my word to get these two to their parents."

Thorias waved a hand in dismissal at the intent behind Hunter's words. "And that honor of yours is why I always stock up on extra bandages and antiseptic when we sojourn off on an expedition."

Moira and Tonks exchanged barely hidden grins. They had witnessed this exchange before. Thorias took his Hippocratic oath as a doctor very seriously. It was as serious as Captain Hunter took his sense of honor.

"Now, Doctor," Hunter began with a sigh.

Interrupting any further conversation aboard the boat, Miles shouted, scrambling over the side of the longskiff to the grass. "Mother!"

Angela, farther back in the boat, cheered for joy and jumped out after him once she saw the pair of adults.

Moira stepped out of the boat and paused next to Hunter, curious to see if her captain needed any help. He noticed her look and shook his head.

"I'll be fine Moira." Hunter explained. "However, I really do appreciate everyone's concern."

Moira shrugged, then turned back to watch the homecoming between Angela, Miles and their parents. It was too far for her to make out what they were saying, but to her, the children were retelling their adventure. The parents looked simply relieved to see their family back together and safe.

"It be good ta see 'em with their ma' and da'." Moira said while she put her hands on her hips. "Good ta have 'em outta harm's way, too."

Captain Hunter steadied himself with his cane and looked over at the scene as Moira watched. "Agreed."

"What of RiBeld?" Tonks asked, joining them. "Ya said he'd vanished before the ship was turned."

Hunter nodded. "That he did."

Thorias snorted in disgust. "Hrmph. Some 'Flower of nobility' RiBeld is. More like 'Rat of the Sewers'. These days, most of the older noble families have squandered anything of value be it money, morality or a sense of honor."

Hunter chuckled, then winced when one of the bullet wounds reminded him he was not fully healed. "He'll return. He may have found a hole to crawl away to, but he'll venture forth when he thinks the storm has passed. The crimes he's committed will not quickly be forgotten. I doubt the Royal Navy will take the charges of murder and piracy against him lightly." The captain sighed. "Either way, he's little more than a nightmare Angela and Miles would do well to forget."

The crew slowly crossed the distance to the campsite. The tent village lay clustered in a wide ring beneath the shelter of birch, pine and popular trees that gave some shelter from the ever-present snow. The tents were canvas with rope bindings that held the tent down at wooden tent pegs driven in through the icy ground. A wide fire pit with a makeshift metal spit dominated the space in the middle of the tents.

At the edge of the tents, a man - in appearance an older version of Miles - tried to wipe soot and dirt from his hands on his brown canvas work trousers. Satisfied most of the grime was gone, he stepped forward and shook hands with each of the crew vigorously. He was easily six feet tall with a thin frame that looked even lankier in his slightly too-large overcoat, white shirt and worn leather shoes.

"It is capital to meet each and all of you. I'm Doctor James Von

Patterson. Angela and Miles were just telling us some of what transpired! It's quite the relief they are unharmed! We'd no idea. Not a single page of correspondence mentioned their flight." The doctor brushed a few stray brown hairs from in front of his eyes.

As Hunter shifted his. The wounds in his side throbbed, leaving him uncomfortable. "Any of your correspondence from an Ian Von Patterson?"

Von Patterson nodded. "Why yes, my brother. He's been looking in upon the family's affairs while I've been away."

Tonks and Moira exchanged a knowing glance. Tonks folded his arms over his chest. "Well then, he's been overseein' things? Your family holds much in the way of property?"

"Just a shipping and trade business. Airship commerce, mind you. Some waterborne travel also." Von Patterson explained. "But what has that got to do with this RiBeld chap?"

The crew exchanged a second glance for a moment. Thorias looked around and sighed. "If none of you speak up, I will. The man has a right to know. It's his own family, after all."

Dr. Von Patterson looked from one crew member to the other. "Would someone please enlighten me. If this involves my family, I daresay it's my right to know."

Hunter cleared his throat. "I'm sorry to say Dr. Von Patterson, that we all have come to believe that your brother, Ian, means your children nothing but harm."

Von Patterson looked stunned, as surely as if physically struck. "What? My brother? I know he can be rather ... harsh ... in his personal affairs but to take action against my children, his own niece and nephew ... it's unthinkable!"

Tonks stepped forward a bit to get Dr. Von Patterson's attention. "Doctor, if ya'll let us, we can explain."

"Please do! I'll have my wife find someone to start tea for us. The conference tent should hold us all." Still shaken by the news, James turned away to speak quietly with his wife, who took the news just as poorly. While she went to locate one of the porters for the expedition, Dr. Von Patterson led the group towards what he considered the 'conference tent'. Near the fire, Hunter paused to catch his breath. Dr. Von Patterson looked back in concern, as did Thorias.

"He's lost a touch of his wind," Thorias explained. "I, too, am a doctor, though more a physician than archeologist. We'll be along in a moment. Tonks, our pilot, knows most of what you need to be told. We'll come to fill in the gaps presently."

"I understand." Dr. Von Patterson replied. "Well then, your tea will be waiting for you."

There by the fire pit, Hunter looked over the ruins and then the mountains beyond. Clouds drifted across the sky, touching the white mountain tops and drawing lazy gray shadows along the snow-covered ground at their feet.

"You appear as a man who wrestles with a quandary," Thorias said idly, pulling his pipe from a coat pocket. Arcady returned from his exploratory flight to land on the doctor's shoulder.

Hunter looked over at the doctor and smiled thinly. He retrieved a worn, soot-stained yellow swatch of cloth from his coat pocket. One side of the cloth was littered with tiny characters in a foreign language and faded ink drawings. "I was reflecting."

"I see." Thorias commented before he withdrew a small pouch of chicory root from another pocket. Deftly, he filled his pipe then put the pouch away. Using a small twig, he knelt and caught it ablaze using what few hot coals remained in the fire pit. He lit his pipe and tossed the twig onto the coals to be consumed.

"A 'prayer flag' is what I'm told this is. It was a gift from the Yeti chieftain, Utawah. It was one of the ones that had hung in his home before we arrived. He said that this one represented long life and good fortune." Captain Hunter explained and showed the cloth to the doctor.

Thorias took a slow puff of his pipe, then exhaled, allowing the smoke to drift upwards in a lazy ring. "Since the chieftain survived, I'd wager they might work."

"I wonder. There were so many that did not. All from one man. Just one single soul." Hunter sighed heavily, as if the weight of the world had suddenly settled on his shoulders.

"RiBeld?" Thorias asked casually.

Hunter shook his head slightly. "No, RiBeld is at best a footnote or epilogue to any tale. A war dog off his leash. I mean Ian Von Patterson."

The doctor nodded, then took another pull on his pipe. The embers in the bowl glowed a gentle orange, casting a warm reflection against Thorias' face. "Anthony, evil ... real evil - not those tawdry tales from the dime novels - doesn't know a number. Some call it a 'bitter fruit' and weed. I daresay 'constrictor vine' or 'inferno' is more spot-on.

If left unchecked, it will take hold and consume anything in its path. Often for the most useless or selfish of goals. Against that, good men and women can only do one thing: stand against it no matter the cost to protect the innocent. Even if it is only one woman, or man."

The sound of laughter rose from off to their right. Twenty feet away Angela and Miles, bundled in warm coats, had tumbled outside in the snow to play and chase each other. Hunter looked at the flag again and smiled. "For the children ... ever vigilant then?"

Thorias smiled slightly. "Unless we wish to be under the heel of the Ian Von Patterson's of the world, I say indeed yes."

Captain Hunter slipped the flag back into his coat pocket and took another deep breath. "We should catch up to the others. Dr. Von Patterson likely might wish to speak to the Royal Navy with us about his brother."
The doctor smiled, and emptied his pipe on the dying coals of the fire pit. "So the hunt is on?"

A shadow of a smile caressed the captain's face. "That is the business of the Royal Navy. However, I'd not be against any consultation they might need."

Epilogue

Evening arrived in London as quietly as an airship drifting into port. The ever famous London fog rose with the evening chill, mingling on the streets with the old soot and smoke of occasional gas lanterns in windows. Clockwork-powered electric street lamps grew obscured, their light diffused and muted, while the fog swirled slowly, methodically among the tight cobblestone streets and few evening pedestrians.

Along the waterfront, the fog held greater reign. There it played madly about, reducing most travelers' visibility to only a few feet along many a winding, twisted 'close' that sat between buildings. Down one of these narrow alleyways a lone figure, dressed in a fine, dark, long wool coat, trousers and shoes paused at an intersection. A cat, startled by the man's sudden appearance, gave a sudden yowl of displeasure and raced off into the night. Similarly startled, the man let out a deep breath, and with shaking hands adjusted his navy blue bowler before he resumed his hurry.

He chose a turn to his right. Ahead, he could make out the dim lanterns of a seedy waterfront pub known locally as Smithy's. The man looked around once more, then confident he had not been observed, slipped around to a side door and inside.

The pub was crowded for a Thursday evening along the waterfront, but not so much that it worried the man. He had greater worries on his mind at that moment. He started to remove his bowler, an automatic reaction to being inside a building, but stopped himself. Others in the pub had not seen fit to do as such, and given his own need for secrecy, he followed their lead. Instead, he unbuttoned his long coat against the comforting warmth of the room and looked around. Across the establishment from him, the person he sought, his longtime business partner, was sitting at a table with a pint of some brewed beverage in front of him. Another pint glass, untouched, was in front of the empty chair there as well. The man who had just entered gently cleared his throat from a bout of nerves, then quietly wound his way through the crowd to the table.

At the table, the man seated there noticed the newcomer, but kept his eye averted. Instead he took a drink and winced. His lip was bruised, eye blackened, and days-old cuts adorned one side of his thin, aristocratic face. A fresh bandage was wrapped around his right hand and wrist, secured tight enough to protect at least one fractured bone or two. Despite the wounds and bandages, he was still well groomed and dressed with a linen shirt, fine captain's coat and well-oiled boots. However, the shirt showed some signs of wear and it hung just a bit loose on his thin frame. It was as if he had lost weight recently due to some malady.

"I thought we intended to meet alone, RiBeld?" The finely dressed man whispered angrily with a sharp, British high-born accent. Even though it was a whisper, his anger made it sound more like a furious hiss.

RiBeld turned a hard and icy stare at the newcomer. "I felt it was prudent to seek out a more public venue. Especially in light of how unexpected our little venture turned out." RiBeld motioned to the chair with the drink in front of it. "Sit down, Ian, you're making a spectacle of yourself, even for this place."

Ian Von Patterson looked around the room nervously, then sat as RiBeld instructed. He returned his angry look to RiBeld. "I am not accustomed to being summoned at your whim like some scullery maid." Von Patterson frowned at RiBeld. "Is there something wrong with you? You look thinner."

RiBeld ignored the comment, took a drink of his ale, and winced again at the dark bruise around his left eye and on his lip that still pained him. With a sigh, he set down the glass and leveled an ugly look at Von Patterson. "Are you bloody well done with your whining? The plan failed. By now I suspect your brother's delightful little spawn are back in his care."

"What?" Von Patterson looked aghast. "Didn't those people I hired locate the wreck? I was assured ..."

"You were assured they were competent at their jobs!" RiBeld interrupted. "Oh and they were. They found the wreck right square away, but then they just wouldn't roll over and die like you assumed. They were a tough lot, tougher than anyone imagined." A faint smirk dashed across RiBeld's face for a moment. "You have to give them at least that, I expect."

"No!" Von Patterson choked on the word as much as he tried not to choke on the explanation given. "I've debts! Mountains of them. With those children dead, my brother would've been held accountable. His shipping business would've come fully under my name. The children's trust fund would've easily covered my debts. Now, I've nothing! I'm ruined! There'll be scandal! Do you know how much I had to pay to bribe the dock-master for the flight plans? What shall I tell my creditors? The Blackheart League! The money I've borrowed from them isn't a small sum."

RiBeld gripped Von Patterson's left arm tight with his own bandaged right hand. Von Patterson whimpered in pain. The mercenary captain pulled the man closer. "Get a hold of yourself and keep your voice down! Now let me make this perfectly and completely clear. Forget about your creditors. They are sheep among the flock. Men hang for what we've done. You have to leave London. Tonight. Take an extended sabbatical. The reach of the Royal Navy and Scotland Yard only goes so far. There are places even they dare not tread."

His thin face ashen, eyes wide with fear, Von Patterson nodded glumly. "Yes, I have to leave... wait, what about the Blackheart League?"

RiBeld released his vice grip on the terrified man next to him. "They'll follow you to the ends of the earth." He said quietly, coldly. "From what I've heard, be of use, and they'll overlook mistakes. While abroad, find some new opportunity for them."

Von Patterson clutched the pint glass in front of him, still full with ale, out of need to hold on to something solid. "And then?"

RiBeld shrugged. "Then if you're lucky, they'll not skin you ... or worse."

Von Patterson swallowed in an attempt to control his heartbeat, which had long ago raced away with itself. He finally nodded silently and stared at the dark, amber-colored drink in front of him.

Just then, a barmaid stopped by their table with a thin smile. She wore her long tresses of brown hair gathered in the back with only a few strands askew to attest to her hours at work. Tired though she was, her eyes lingered on the glowering form of RiBeld and the pale, thin, terrified looks of Von Patterson. She had worked at Smithy's for many years. Enough to know dark dealings when she saw them. Especially when it was dark dealings gone horribly awry. Those were sights one never spoke about, that is, if one wished to continue to draw breath another day.

"'Ere now. A right smart stout for ya both." She set down two pint glasses filled with a charcoal-dark stout covered atop with a rich white foam.

The two men exchanged a glance. RiBeld was the first to look up.

"These are not ours. You're at the wrong table." He said flatly.

The barmaid shrugged. "Nevva said ya did, 'guv. Drinks are from the guvnor o'er in the corner." She nodded in the direction of the far corner of the room.

RiBeld's eyes darted to where she indicated, but the corner was dark and the room crowded. For Von Patterson, however, that was the breaking point. He rose quickly, nearly spilling both ale and stout over the table and bumping into the barmaid. RiBeld had been so intent on looking for who their mysterious benefactor was he missed his chance to grab the panicked Von Patterson.

"Von Patterson! Sit down! You're making a spectacle!" RiBeld hissed furiously.

Von Patterson backed away from the table. "You're quite right you know, a long trip. A quite long one. It will do the nerves good." The man stammered. His hands shook uncontrollably while he pushed his way for the door. RiBeld rose and took one last look at the corner.

There, from the gloom, a figure rose from its chair. Dressed in a worn leather long coat, hair cropped neat and short in the Royal Navy style, Captain Anthony Hunter leaned on his cane a moment before taking a step forward into the lamp light. A small smile crossed his face as he inclined his head slightly to RiBeld in a silent greeting.

The mercenary captain spun about in a panic to grab Von Patterson, but the man was nearly to the door. He pushed the barmaid aside and shoved his way after Von Patterson before things could grow worse.

Ian Von Patterson almost laughed nervously to himself. He would get away and hide. No one would find him. He would be safe. He reached for the front door just as a broad-shouldered man dressed in brown tweed trousers, jacket and cream linen shirt stepped up in front of him.

"Ian Von Patterson, I presume?" The man asked curtly.

an paused, his thoughts derailed. The man's manner of dress fit that of a common dock worker. His speech was anything but. "Yes?" He stammered to reply through his fog of confusion.

The man nodded to someone outside of Von Patterson's view. "You'll come with us now, Sirrah." Behind Von Patterson another man, similarly dressed, stepped up.

Panic suddenly galvanized Ian's thoughts. "Wait, no! What is this?"

RiBeld appeared next to the trio at that moment. "Back off. Find someone else to pinch for money!" He growled at the two men.

The man at the door was not in the least flustered. He looked over at RiBeld with a raised eyebrow. "That's 'Constable' to you ... Archibald RiBeld is it?"

It was RiBeld's turn to grow pale when the other constable, similarly disguised, grabbed onto both RiBeld and Von Patterson. "Come along quiet now. There's an Inspector quite anxious to have a bit of a chat with the two of you over the matter of a shipwreck."

Von Patterson went limp, whimpering, but RiBeld was not so easily taken. Immediately, he punched the constable in front of him, then turned on the one behind. Quickly, the door burst open and four more constables, dressed in uniform rushed into the panic of the pub to lunge for RiBeld. Behind them walked two men in suits and long coats. Hunter limped slowly over to one these, a man in his late forties with short graying hair and a stout frame that filled his brown tweed suit.

"Inspector Kincade." Hunter said pleasantly.

"Good evening to you, Captain Hunter. It seems your information was indeed correct." The police inspector said with a smile. "Given your accusations, it was a hard story to believe. But it seems to be quite true given what we've overheard so far."

With great interest, Hunter was watching the fight between RiBeld and the police that had just now finished, with RiBeld the loser. "Quite, indeed. I'm only glad you were willing to humor me in this."

"Well, a charge of murder and attempted murder alone is

enough to merit attention, despite the other fantastic claims you made. We're in your debt on this." He offered his hand to the captain.

Hunter accepted it and shook it briefly. "The thanks are appreciated, Inspector, but they may be somewhat premature."

"How do you mean?"

Hunter pointed at the bloody, growling visage of RiBeld. "That isn't Archibald RiBeld."

"What?" Von Patterson screeched, confusion and panic evident in his eyes. "I've been set up!"

"Quiet you." Growled the constable.

Von Patterson looked about, eyes wild. "They cannot get me. What they will do will be horror. I cannot be found."

The constable pulled Von Patterson a short distance away with another order for the man to control himself.

The inspector looked incredulous at Hunter's statement. "Preposterous! I've seen the man myself. I've met him through state functions many times, and he is here as you said he'd be."

"Be that as it may, and I daresay I don't know how he pulled it off to look so near perfect, that man there is only disguised as RiBeld. Let me offer you proof." Hunter walked forward towards RiBeld, who glared daggers at Hunter.

The captain pointed at RiBeld's right hand. "When he and I last met, I broke his right wrist in the fight with my left hand." Hunter tugged the glove off his left hand to reveal the intricate brass and leather artificial clockwork hand underneath. The gears turned methodically with a dull whir and click. "We watched that man lift a glass and grab Von Patterson with that very same right hand. If broken, he shouldn't be able to do that, and if healed by some strange arcane means, there would at least be a scar or a faint residue from the process. He must likewise be wearing a disguise."

Kincade considered this a moment. "Loosen the man's wrappings. Just enough to see this."

The nearest constable nodded and reached for RiBeld's bandaged right hand. The man's eyes went wide with fury and panic. In a surge of strength, he shoved the constables aside and lunged for Hunter. "I'll kill you!"

Hunter backed away, but not quick enough. RiBeld slammed into the captain and the pair smashed into a table, spilling drinks across the pub. Immediately behind them two constables lunged to recover RiBeld. Inspector Kincade likewise grabbed for the man.

In the fight, the bandages had come loose. Instead of revealing a scar, broken skin or bruise, his wrist was completely undamaged. The inspector frowned. "Well, this is most unusual. Not a hint of a scar or any sign of a break. However, if you do have the likeness of RiBeld, so you'll be coming to the Yard with us for quite a long chat anyway. We'll have a specialist come around to check you for any arcane healing you might have gotten, 'Archibald RiBeld' or whatever your name really is."

"Inspector," one of the constables who held the fake RiBeld said. "Best take a look here."

The constable tightened his grip and forced RiBeld's head to one side. There, just barely visible under some well-applied stage makeup, was what appeared to be a seam sewn into the man's skin.

Hunter stepped back in shock, eyes wide while Inspector Kincade gasped.

"Just what are you?" Kincade asked astounded.

"Nothing any of you will comprehend!" The fake RiBeld snarled, an insane rage boiling behind his eyes. "They'll come for you, all of you!"

Slowly, the constables led out the whimpering Von Patterson from the pub. Behind them, the fake RiBeld was bodily hauled away, all the while hurling insults and curses at both Hunter and Kincade.

"So the villain remains at large, eh? Unfortunate, that." Inspector Kincade said solemnly with a sigh to regain his composure. "All of this only tightens the noose on his neck. We'll see what we can glean from the impostor, including what he actually might even be. If we're fortunate, we'll have the real RiBeld in hand soon enough. It seems he's much to answer for here. As much as Von Patterson."

"Equally so, Inspector, equally so." Hunter commented.

Kincade nodded, then stuck out his hand again. "Quite. Be that as it may, thank you again for the assist. We may have some questions for you as well, since you and your crew were witnesses as much as victims of this."

"We've only put into port here. We'll be available for many days yet. Just send word and we'll be at your disposal." Hunter said while he shook the inspector's hand again.

"Good man. Well, good evening to you then." Kincade said before he vanished through the door.

Hunter followed along silently. Outside, he paused beneath the sole street lamp of Smithy's pub. The muted click of clockwork mechanics and gears echoed in the air. A dull, yellow light shone around, muted by the fog and soot of the close. He withdrew a crumpled piece of paper from his pocket. It had been shoved there when he struggled with the fake RiBeld. He had not felt when it happened, only that it was suddenly there after the scuffle had finished. He replaced the glove over his clockwork hand and slowly opened the note.

"Oh captain, my captain,

The true game is about to begin.

We are not nearly done with our 'dance'.

A. RiBeld,

Blackheart League"

Hunter frowned and closed a fist around the note. The chill from a sudden updraft of wind blew off the waterfront with its smell of stale fish.

"Then let the game begin."

About the Author

C. B. Ash holds degrees as a Physical Scientist and Computer Scientist. Since college, he has run his own networking business, worked as laboratory technician, taught martial arts, and traveled for several years as a software engineering consultant.

During that time he has written several fantasy and science fiction short stories, a fantasy/murder mystery novel and several poems. One of which garnered him the Emily Dickinson Award in Poetry. His first novel, *Kinloch*, was published in May, 2004. *Tales of the Brass Griffin: A Children's Tale* is in the *Tales of the Brass Griffin* series. To find out more, visit: http://BrassGriffin.com.